LØRD ØF
HØRSES

H. L. Macfarlane

COPYRIGHT

DEDICATION

For dark mirrors and darker lochs.

THE KELPIE

Folk alone in lonely lanes
Gladly take the horse's reins,
Innocence the creature feigns
Then takes the rider down
To the loch-side so remote;
The rider who the Kelpie caught
Is murdered now without a thought;
In icy loch they drown.
The Kelpie (N. Baker; 2010)

CHAPTER ONE

Murdoch

Murdoch loved the water more than anything, and he adored the loch he lived in most of all.

Spending two years banished to the bottom of it by the golden faerie king and his ice-blue queen changed his perspective on things.

In truth Murdoch wasn't even Murdoch. He'd taken the unfortunate Mister Buchanan's name, as well as his face and memories, when he'd dragged the man down into the loch and consumed his body and soul. But Murdoch didn't have the guise of the human anymore; without his bridle he could not change his form at all.

He liked the man's name, though, so even now he kept it.

For months Murdoch glowered and mulled and rued his fate at the very bottom of Loch Lomond. There was nothing else he could do, after all. If he dared show up at the surface and was spied by a damned faerie then his bridle would be destroyed, and Murdoch would have no chance of ever recovering his full powers again.

He'd had no intention of risking his very existence by leaving the depths of the loch. He truly hadn't. That was, until Murdoch heard something that changed his priorities entirely.

For there were plans to fill in the shallow, southern shores of his home, funded by the very company Murdoch Buchanan himself had worked for, before the kelpie had devoured him. He had to do something to stop the plan. If he didn't then he would not be the only one who suffered.

He desperately needed to talk to Sorcha Darrow.

It hadn't been easy, finding a way through which he could reach her. Murdoch could not come galloping out of the loch in his true form to find her; he would be far too conspicuous, and if a wary local attacked him with silver then he would die.

Murdoch had hoped Sorcha would come into the loch to swim. That way, without raising any suspicion, he could talk to her. But the first summer after his banishment she did not so much as dip her toes in the water, and the second she seemed to avoid even coming down to the shore.

I have ruined things with her, Murdoch despaired on more than one occasion. *I should have told her that I would love to speak to her again. She must be so afraid.*

And so, with no easy way to tell Sorcha about what was going on, Murdoch had to find another way to allow him to walk upon land unnoticed. Luckily for him, the very creatures infesting the loch that had caused Murdoch to try and destroy the faerie realms and, in

4

turn, landed him in his current, powerless state, were the answer to his problems.

The Unseelie.

Murdoch hunted, ensnared and consumed every dark, sly, creeping faerie that had sought to make Loch Lomond their new home. With every drop of blood spilled he learned more and more of how their magic worked until, when autumn was truly turning into winter, Murdoch discovered where an Unseelie creature strong enough to help him resided – in his own home.

"Why should I help a kelpie?" the ill-begotten ghoul asked when Murdoch found it. Its murky, midnight-coloured hair swirled around its face like dead weeds, and its silvered skin shone akin to fish scales in the water. When it grinned Murdoch saw a set of sharp, broken teeth that had clearly been used to rend through flesh and bone.

"You like my home," Murdoch countered. "You revel in lost souls, just as I do. If you help me then I will not kill you where you stand, and you will be free to live out your days here with no further danger from me."

The creature laughed an ugly, garbled laugh. "You water folk can lie. I know you can. So how can I trust this deal you are suggesting?"

Murdoch solidified his ghostly, insubstantial form until he could tear open his flesh upon his own teeth, which were even sharper than the Unseelie's. His blood darkened the water; the faerie's odd, metallic eyes gleamed at the sight of it.

"A blood pact will ensure we both keep our sides of the bargain," Murdoch said. "Is that enough to gain your trust?"

"Then what is it that you want?" the Unseelie asked, lapping up Murdoch's blood with a forked tongue as it spoke.

"I wish to take on the form of a human. There is someone I need to see."

"That is some tough magic. Where is your bridle?"

Murdoch pawed at the sandy loch floor in frustration. "Currently indisposed. Will you help me or not?"

The creature stared at him, unblinking, for a long time. Eventually it said, "Twelve hours. That is all I can give you, so that is all you will have."

"Deal," Murdoch replied, heartbeat quickening in earnest. With this he would finally be able to talk to Sorcha, though convincing her to take back his bridle from her Seelie prince would be no easy task. Twelve hours really was no time at all.

Twelve hours would have to be enough.

The creature grinned. With a sharp nail it cut open the palm of its hand, smearing the silver-blue blood that spilled from its wound across Murdoch's forehead. "The moment you surface you will be transformed," it warned, "so do not break through the loch until you are where you need to be."

Wordlessly, Murdoch dissolved into the loch and used underwater currents to help speed up his journey to its southern shores, where the hamlet of Darach - and Sorcha Darrow's house - was. *I will have to appear as Murdoch Buchanan,* he realised as he neared the shore. *She will not recognise anyone else, and her parents would not let anyone they do not know into their house.*

The thought of Sorcha's parents gave Murdoch

pause. He hadn't considered how to handle them upon reaching the Darrow household. Ultimately deciding that he would cross that bridge when he came to it, Murdoch closed his eyes as he reached the upper layer of the loch, broke through the surface and –

Inhaled the ice-cold night air deeply into a pair of unfamiliar, human lungs. He swam the last fifty feet to the shore, wobbling unsteadily on legs that had not been used to walk for a long, long time. A gigantic shiver wracked Murdoch's body.

"It is f-freezing," he muttered, running his hands up and down his arms as he got his bearings. A strong gust of wind blew a load of wet, bitter snow into his face; Murdoch sneezed and cowered from the next lot before it could sting his eyes again.

I need clothes, Murdoch realised as he staggered across the sand. *I cannot show up to the Darrow house completely naked.*

But it quickly became apparent that Murdoch had no other choice. The weather was so brutal not a single clothes line was hanging up outside, and the MacPherson farm's barn and outbuildings were firmly locked and bolted against the wind.

"How do I explain all this to Sorcha?" Murdoch screamed into the wind, beyond frustrated that such a simple, stupid problem as needing *clothes* was wasting so much of his precious time. He stomped and slid through mud and slush until he spied her house, mind drawing a complete blank for the words to tell her what exactly was going on.

Just go up to the front door and knock, Murdoch thought. *There is no other way around it. Be thankful you have this opportunity at all. Do not waste it.*

7

When Murdoch finally crept along the gravelled pathway to the Darrow house he noticed that their carriage was missing, and that Sorcha's parents' room – as well as her father's study – was dark. Not daring to believe that he had managed to stumble across Sorcha when she was completely alone, Murdoch ran a hand through his dark, sodden hair and breathed deeply through his nose.

This is it, he told himself as he held a fist up to the front door. *She hasn't seen you in two years. She probably believes she'd never see you again – probably doesn't want to see you again.*

For the sake of both their homes Murdoch had to ignore the stinging in his heart at the thought of Sorcha trying to push him away. And so, with an overwhelming sense of fear washing over him, Murdoch knocked on the door...just as it was flung open.

Sorcha stood in the doorway, bucket of water in her hands. It came crashing and clattering to the floor as soon as she saw Murdoch, dripping wet and naked, standing a mere foot away from her.

He risked a smile, though his frozen muscles protested strongly against it.

"Miss Darrow," he said, inclining his head politely. "It has been too long."

CHAPTER TWO

Lachlan

"...Lachlan. Lachlan? _Lachlan!_"

"...what is it?"

Lachlan's gaze slid lazily over to Ailith. He had been dozing on the throne, he knew, but he did not care. The day had been long and dark and dreary, and all he wanted was a jug of wine and his bed.

And a song.

Ailith tutted, delicately crossing her legs on the ornate throne that had been built for her when she had become Lachlan's queen. "If you do not wish to discuss this now it can wait until the morrow," she said, "but it cannot be delayed any longer than that. Things are tense enough with the Unseelie as it is without you ignoring Eirian's emissaries."

"Then let said emissaries wait until tomorrow," Lachan drawled. "Given what the Unseelie king's brethren tried to do to me they can bloody wait another day."

His ice-blonde queen sighed patiently. "If he was going to wage war to avenge his brother and nephew he'd have made that clear already."

"Would he? The Unseelie are known for their deceptiveness, even to us. He might be waiting."

"For what?"

"...I do not know," Lachlan admitted, turning from Ailith in the process.

Life had been hard-going for Lachlan during the past two years. As if being cursed to live as a fox by his stepfather and stepbrother hadn't been enough for him to deal with, the fallout from a *kelpie* having posed as the Golden Prince of Faeries to assassinate both traitorous Unseelies had left Lachlan with utter pandemonium within his realm to calm and control. The creature had drowned fifteen members of the Seelie Court in its rampage, all to incite a war between the two faerie factions.

And steal Sorcha Darrow in the process.

It was Lachlan's turn to sigh. He hadn't seen Sorcha for two months, his work as king having taken up too much of his time to visit her. And Sorcha was working hard herself – her father's health had deteriorated so much that both he and her mother had moved to Glasgow to be closer to a respectable doctor. That left Sorcha to take up her father's business: looking after the land that surrounded Loch Lomond and the people that lived upon it.

For the hundredth time, Lachlan wished Sorcha had accepted his offer to live with him in the Seelie Court. He missed her dearly, and felt uneasy about how close she was to the loch. Lachlan may have cast the kelpie back from whence it came – and promised to destroy its bridle should it dare resurface again – but that didn't mean Lachlan trusted his threat would be enough to keep the creature away from Sorcha.

It loved her, after all.

"You are thinking of Miss Sorcha, aren't you?" Ailith asked, a knowing smile on her face.

Lachlan rolled his eyes. "Don't give me that look."

"I never thought I would see the day that you were so interested in a human, Lachlan," she laughed. "And for two years, no less! I must admit, I thought you would have lost interest in her by now. I am glad that you have proved me wrong."

"Why, because it means you get to watch me suffer?"

She slapped his arm gently. "You are so over-dramatic."

"I know. You love it."

"Is there really no way Miss Sorcha can be convinced to live as one of us?" Ailith wondered aloud for both herself and Lachlan. "Surely things are different for her now. A lot can change for a human in two years."

"She has more responsibilities now, certainly," he complained. "Though that only seems to make her want to remain exactly the way she is even more. Damn mortal sensibilities."

Neither of them said anything for a minute or two, their silence punctuated only by the arrival of a servant proffering them a bronze tray with two goblets of wine upon it. Both Lachlan and Ailith happily took one each.

After a long draught of the heady, crimson liquid,

Lachlan slumped even deeper into his throne. "Winter is boring," he moaned. "Hardly anyone comes into the forest. No humans lurking and searching, wishing to make a deal with a faerie, or seeking a revel, or searching for a whisper of a soul already lost to us."

Ailith squeezed his hand. "It has always been this way in the weeks leading to the winter solstice."

"Yes, but before I was king I could come and go as I please, seeking out mischief wherever I went. Now I must stay here...ruling. How did my mother ever manage it? It is suffocating."

"Maybe so, but you are good at it," Ailith reassured. "You are proving those wrong who believed that you were not ready."

"Too bad the lead perpetrators are too *dead* to see that they were wrong," Lachlan muttered darkly.

Ailith said nothing. She did not like to talk about Queen Evanna's second husband, the half-Unseelie Innis, nor of the faerie's son, Fergus. She had been engaged to marry Fergus, after all, though she had not agreed to the union out of love. But she clearly had some feelings that remained for her tempestuous husband-to-be, even after discovering he had been the one who cursed Lachlan.

Just as Sorcha still has feelings for the kelpie, though she would never admit to it.

For it did not matter that Sorcha delighted in seeing Lachlan whenever they managed to snatch a few hours of time together, nor that all they thought of was each other during those hours. Sorcha was alone with the loch right outside her door, and Lachlan had seen the way she looked out across it when she thought nobody was watching.

It tore Lachlan apart with jealousy.

"Speaking of the solstice," Ailith said, magicking a thick, silvery card out of thin air to spin it between her hands, "you still haven't responded to Eirian's invitation to the winter revel. You know you must go."

Lachlan made a face. "What is wrong with us having our own one? Why must he hold dominion over all things dark and frozen?"

"Because you get to hold the revel during the summer solstice, and it is only fair." Ailith threw the invitation at Lachlan, who caught it without looking at it. Sighing heavily, he pressed his thumbprint against the card and closed his eyes. When he opened them again the invitation was gone.

He made a face at Ailith. "There. It is done. Are you happy n-"

"King Lachlan," a frantic-looking, red-faced Seelie with the ears and antlers of a young buck announced as it skittered across the throne room, startling Lachlan out of his bad mood. Both he and Ailith perked up at the intrusion.

"What is it?" she asked.

The creature shifted on the spot uncomfortably. Lachlan's heart rate sped up; something told him he would not like what he was about to hear.

"You said you wished to be informed the moment the - the moment the kelpie emerged from the loch," they stammered. "I saw a man swimming out of the water down on the southern shore, and it looked -"

"A *man*?"

The buck nodded.

"Then it could not be the kelpie," Ailith said, smiling warmly for the trembling Seelie. "But thank you for your information –"

"No, it looked like – I was there when the kelpie tried to d-drown us all," they insisted. "This man looked just like the guise the monster took two years ago."

Lachlan's face darkened. "The southern shore of the loch, you say? Did you see where the man was headed?"

The creature looked too terrified to reply. Lachlan knew that he cut an intimidating figure, particularly now that his magical powers increased with every day he sat upon the Seelie throne. Even draped across said throne in a half-undone shirt, breeches and no shoes he had the capacity to incite fear in those he faced.

He was not in the mood to dull his presence for the sake of a quivering faun.

"Where was he headed?" Lachlan asked again, voice full of warning. "You must tell me."

The creature gulped.

"Miss Darrow's house."

Lachlan stared at Ailith, who stared right back at him. In her haunting blue eyes Lachlan could see his own face, golden and livid and full of a fear he would never admit to.

Am I stronger than the kelpie now? Can I end his life where I could not before?

"Time to pay Sorcha a visit," Lachlan said, a vicious, vulpine snarl curling his lips.

There was only one way to find out.

14

CHAPTER THREE

Sorcha

Sorcha couldn't believe her eyes. She simply couldn't. For there was no way Murdoch Buchanan was standing on the threshold of her house, his dark hair dripping glacial water down his ghostly-pale, naked skin.

Very, very naked skin, Sorcha thought, forcing her eyes back up the man's face as soon as she realised they had wandered downward.

"Can I come in?" Murdoch asked. Sorcha became aware of the fact that he'd already asked the question twice already, and all she'd done was stare blankly at him. He was shivering and shaking; clearly he had been wandering around outside for a while.

Sorcha numbly waved Murdoch inside, forcing the heavy wooden door shut behind him to keep out the howling storm threatening to blow snow down the hallway. She stumbled along to the parlour room – where she had been sitting by the fire to read a book – and yanked open a chest of drawers to pull out a large, tartan blanket.

She flung it at Murdoch.

"You – what is this?" Sorcha asked, so quietly she could barely hear herself over the crackling of the fire. She didn't dare to look at him. "Are you...are you –"

"The kelpie, yes," Murdoch coughed. He wrapped the blanket around himself, waiting until Sorcha indicated for him to sit by the fire with a panicky jolt of her head to fall to the carpeted floor. "We both know the real Murdoch is dead."

Sorcha was torn between collapsing onto the armchair by the hearth and pacing back and forth in distress. In the end she perched upon the very edge of the chair, back stock straight as she stared down at the shivering figure of Murdoch Buchanan wrapped in a blanket.

His hair has grown longer, Sorcha thought when she noticed the way it almost reached his shoulders. *How could that be possible? The kelpie is merely borrowing the man's form to – to –*

"How are you human?" she demanded, finally vocalising the first question she should have asked the very moment she saw Murdoch standing outside her door.

The kelpie's impossibly dark eyes bored into her own. There were deep-set shadows beneath them; along with the hollowness of his cheeks Murdoch looked altogether haunted. *Or dead, which the man himself has long-since been.*

Sorcha pushed the disturbing thought away.

"I made a deal with an Unseelie ghoul," he explained, though his voice was so cracked Sorcha barely

16

understood him. With a swish of her dress she got to her feet, waving for Murdoch to stay exactly where he was in the process.

"I'll get you some water," she said, "and food. You look half-starved."

The smallest of smiles quirked his lips. "That will happen, when all you eat for months and months are the lowest of the fae."

Sorcha did not respond. She did not know how.

She took her time in the kitchen, browsing through the pantry to locate cheese, oatcakes and some salted ham her parents had brought back from Glasgow a few days prior. Alongside these Sorcha filled a cup with water that had been boiled over the fire an hour ago; it was pleasantly warm to the touch. She added a dash of honey to it to help ease Murdoch's throat.

Lastly Sorcha threw a few cubes of tablet that she had made the evening before for lack of anything better to do. It still didn't have the texture her mother's tablet had, but she was getting better and better at making the sugary confection with every new attempt.

And then, because it would not do to stall any further, Sorcha placed everything onto a wooden tray and brought it back through to the parlour room. Murdoch was staring at the fire as he warmed his hands against it, though when he heard Sorcha's footsteps he turned to smile at her.

He does not look angry with me, she thought. *Even after what I did to him. How could that be?*

Sorcha placed the tray of food down on the floor in front of Murdoch before sitting opposite him. "I apologise," she said, "I didn't have any leftovers from dinner, so cold meat and cheese will have to do."

But Murdoch shook his head at Sorcha's apology. "I did not expect you to feed me, Miss Darrow. This is far more than I deserve." He picked up the cup of honeyed water, sighing contentedly when the liquid passed his lips.

"...you said you made a deal with an Unseelie," Sorcha ventured, curiosity finally overcoming her need to be a gracious host. The kelpie was hardly her usual kind of house guest, after all. "Are you – does that mean you can change your form again?"

Murdoch gulped down a mouthful of cheese before replying. He glanced at the ornately carved, oak-wood clock hanging on the wall. "I have another ten hours in this skin, or thereabouts. When my time is up I will return back to the way I was before."

"Then why...what are you doing here? What do you need?"

"Miss Darrow..." Murdoch held her gaze for a long moment then cast his eyes downward. "I need my bridle back. But it is not to do anything nefarious, I swear. I need to go to London."

London?

Of all the answers the kelpie could have given, this was the last one Sorcha had expected. She slid from the armchair to kneel in front of Murdoch. "What is in London?" she asked. "Just what is wrong?"

"Grey and MacKinnon – the company Murdoch Buchanan still officially works for – have grown impatient with his extended stay up here, Miss Darrow."

A pause. It did not take Sorcha long to work out what Murdoch meant. "...they want to do something with the land around the loch again, don't they?" she said. "How have you been holding them off for so long in the first place? You were – I mean, you aren't actually *Mr Buchanan*."

Murdoch laughed humourlessly. "No, I am not, but considering I planned to use this appearance to ensure no harm was wrought on my home, I had certain countermeasures put in place before I went searching for my runaway bride two years ago."

Sorcha blushed before she could stop herself. She looked away. "What kind of countermeasures?" she mumbled, twisting her hands in her lap as she did so.

"Everyone in London believes that you and Mr Buchanan have spent the last two years enjoying an extended engagement. It has held the company off until now, but I'm afraid the time I managed to borrow has been spent. Miss Darrow, they intend to fill in the shallowest southern shores of the loch to make room for official hunting and holiday lodges."

"They *what*?!"

Gone was Sorcha's previous wariness of Murdoch; with a furious expression on her face she pushed away the tray of food that separated them and leaned towards him, hands balanced on Murdoch's knees to keep her from falling over. He seemed entirely surprised by her sudden closeness, though Sorcha did not have it in her to care right now.

"I own the land around here!" she shouted at him. "My father signed it over to me last year so they could not bully him into handing it over! They cannot walk onto *my land* and –"

Murdoch cupped Sorcha's face between his hands,

silencing her tirade prematurely. There was a softness in his eyes that Sorcha had dreamed about more often than she dared to admit, not least because the kelpie had looked at her with the same exact expression transforming his features before she had ripped his bridle away from him.

And broken his heart.

"Miss Darrow," he said, an agonisingly fond smile upon his lips, "I plan to stop them, rest assured. But for that, I need to beg of you a favour." He inhaled deeply through his nose. "Is there any way I can convince you to ask your golden faerie for my bridle back?"

Sorcha froze. Murdoch seemed to take this as a *no,* for the smile fell from his face and he made to drop his hands. But Sorcha raised her own to keep them there, instead, and in doing so lost her balance. When she began to fall towards Murdoch's chest his grip tightened on her face to keep her upright.

"There is no need for me to do such a thing," Sorcha said, laughing giddily. Her heart was beating so hard and fast it felt as if it would burst from her chest; she had not felt this alive in months.

Murdoch frowned, confused by both Sorcha's answer and their new-found proximity. "...what do you mean, Miss Darrow?" he asked, very quietly.

She grinned. "Lachlan does not have your bridle. I do; it is mine."

It took a few moments for the truth of what Sorcha had said to sink in for Murdoch. His frown deepened, and then disappeared, and he ran a hand through Sorcha's hair to bring her even closer to him.

Sorcha hardly dared to breathe. The air between her

and the kelpie was dark and electric – an achingly familiar, dangerously seductive atmosphere that Sorcha had been sure she'd never feel wash over her again.

She leaned into his touch just a little more.

"You would let me have it?" Murdoch asked, voice low and melodic and full of hope.

Of course Sorcha was going to let him have it. She had never wanted to take it from him in the first place.

Her lips parted. "Ye–"

"Absolutely not."

Murdoch and Sorcha's eyes widened in unison. They turned their heads to face the door. For there stood Lachlan, as thunderous and wild as the storm currently battering the Darrow household.

A growl leapt from his lips. "Get away from Clara or so help you, kelpie, I shall destroy you where you stand."

CHAPTER FOUR

Murdoch

"Do I have to repeat myself, you bloody horse?" Lachlan fired at Murdoch. "Get away from her - *now.*"

But Murdoch did not move. How could he? Sorcha Darrow was in his arms. She was in his arms, and she had his bridle, and she wanted to give it back to him. Her passion to protect her home - *their home* - had ignited her mismatched eyes like fire.

He would never willingly let that go.

But then Sorcha shifted away from him, and the spell was broken.

"Lachlan," she said, standing up to greet him with a wary smile on her face, "once you have heard what is going on you will understand why I wish to give him his bridle back."

"That *monster* was told not to resurface!" the faerie snarled, ire dripping from every syllable he spoke. He glared at Murdoch. "But you just had to see her, didn't you? You couldn't leave her well enough alone. And you have the gall to demand she help you? Why would you ever think that –"

Sorcha slapped him.

"If you do not *listen*, Lachlan," she warned, "then I will give Murdoch back his bridle without so much as including you in the conversation. Are we clear?"

Murdoch did not think he could love Sorcha Darrow more than he already did, but he was blissfully, painfully wrong. Watching a human have the power to physically harm a faerie with no repercussions was immensely satisfying, especially when said faerie was the Seelie king.

Lachlan was positively stunned by both Sorcha's slap and her threat. Clearly he did not know what to say, torn between incandescent rage and disbelief as he was.

"Miss Sorcha, it is good to see you...despite the circumstances," came a soft, feminine voice from the doorway. Murdoch stood up, wrapping the tartan blanket Sorcha had given him a little tighter around his body in the process. For there was Ailith, the beautiful faerie who had become Lachlan's queen after he ascended the throne.

The one who loved Lachlan with all her heart, yet had decided to break his anyway. The one who was responsible for Lachlan seeking to enchant Sorcha into being his until the end of time.

Sorcha rushed over to embrace the female faerie, who happily reciprocated the gesture. She kissed Sorcha's brow, then pulled away from her to give Murdoch a once-over. "You do not look well, kelpie," she said. "How is it that you appear before us as the late Mr Buchanan once more?"

Murdoch took a moment to inhale the heady woodsmoke emitted from the fireplace before he spoke; the smell helped to ground him. For he did *not* feel well, not at all. Clearly the Unseelie ghoul's magic did not agree with him in the slightest.

"I made a deal with a darker fae," he explained for Ailith's benefit, and Lachlan's. "I have another ten or so hours left before their magic wears off."

Lachlan barked at the explanation, sounding entirely like the fox he had once been. "An Unseelie was foolish enough to help the creature that killed its own kin?"

"Given that they were skulking in Loch Lomond I somehow doubt they care much for their brethren," Murdoch countered. "Or they do not wish to be found by said kin." That was how most fae - Seelie and Unseelie alike - ended up hiding underwater, after all.

"And what was *so important* that you had to make a deal with their kind in order to show up at Clara's door?"

"Why don't you sit down, Lachlan, and he can tell you," Sorcha cut in, gesturing for both Lachlan and Ailith to sit upon the armchairs by the parlour room's bay window, which overlooked the loch. Once upon a time Murdoch had sat there with Sorcha to have their first real conversation, and he had teased and scared her.

It felt like forever ago.

It was Ailith who sat down first, giving Lachlan a pointed look until he, too, collapsed onto the chair beside her with a scowl on his face.

"Fine," the faerie muttered. "Explain away, kelpie, whilst I am in the mood to listen."

And so Murdoch told the King and Queen of the

Seelie Court all about Grey and MacKinnon, and the looming threat the company posed to the Darrow land. Sorcha fussed around them, pouring drams of pale amber whisky and topping up Murdoch's cup of honeyed water.

When Murdoch's explanation came to an end nobody spoke for a few minutes. Clearly Lachlan and Ailith were mulling over what he had told them, though with every passing second Sorcha grew more and more restless. She sat on her armchair, then stoked the fire, then wandered over to a chest of drawers to rearrange the contents. Murdoch was tempted to pull her down to sit on the floor beside him; it took everything in him to resist doing so.

Eventually, Lachlan turned his golden eyes on Murdoch and said, "There is no way I am allowing you to travel *anywhere* with your full powers unsupervised."

"He won't be unsupervised," Sorcha said. Everyone stared at her as she finished refolding a blanket that did not need refolding.

"What do you mean, Miss Darrow?" Murdoch asked, just as curious as Lachlan and Ailith were.

She straightened her back and cleared her throat. "I'm going with you, of course."

"Absolutely not!"

"But it makes sense, Lachlan," Sorcha countered, silencing the faerie with a single glance. She twisted her hair over one shoulder with her fidgeting, restless hands. She was nervous, that much was apparent, but Sorcha also had a determined expression on her face which told Murdoch she had resolutely made up her mind.

"I am meant to be engaged to Mr Buchanan," she

said. "Grey and MacKinnon believe he has spent the last two years up here living with me. It would be better for me to travel down to London with Murdoch to meet the man's associates. That way I can keep track of what is actually going on...as well as ensuring the kelpie does not get up to no good."

Lachlan looked as if he desperately wished to complain. Murdoch himself was torn between protesting Sorcha's suggestion and gleefully accepting it. For there was no doubt Mr Buchanan's associates had few qualms with stooping low and using questionable methods to acquire things they wanted, going by the man's memories. It would be dangerous to put Sorcha in front of them. But on the other hand...

I would get to spend time with her by myself, with no fox-cursed faeries getting in our way.

When Lachlan stood up Ailith followed suit. He took her hand and raised it to his lips, then let it go in order to face Sorcha. "We need to talk, Clara," he said, temper clearly barely contained. He fired another glare at Murdoch. "In private."

She nodded, sparing Murdoch a glance before following Lachlan out of the parlour room. Murdoch and Ailith sat in awkward, agonised silence punctuated only by the snap and crackle of the fire and the roaring storm unsettling Loch Lomond outside the curtained window.

"So you wed him," Murdoch murmured, simply to break the unbearable tension. He kept his eyes on the fox-orange flames blackening the stone hearth. "You really did love him; that was not a lie."

"You know my kind cannot lie," Ailith said. "I have always loved Lachlan."

"If that is the case then why do you appear unperturbed by his feelings for Miss Darrow?"

She let out an impassioned sigh. "There is so much you do not understand, kelpie. Your solitary life has left you woefully ignorant."

Murdoch bristled at Ailith's comment, though her tone had not been patronising – she had simply spoken something which she believed to be the truth.

He scowled at her. "And what does that mean, exactly?"

"It means that the Seelie are not constrained by such restrictive notions as monogamy. It is possible for us to love more than one soul at a time, and deeply. You rarely hear of faeries slaughtering one another in jealous rages; this is why."

"That may work well for you," Murdoch countered, "but Miss Darrow is human. She –"

"Has been more than happy with her and Lachlan's arrangement up to now," the faerie interrupted, "though it is clear from your face that you do not wish to acknowledge that."

Murdoch had no reply.

"Although," Ailith added on, voice very soft. She pulled aside the curtain to stare into the dark, unruly night with almost vacant eyes. "I do believe Lachlan would throw me aside if Sorcha asked him to. If Sorcha accepted his offer."

"If she...what has he offered her?"

Ailith's laugh was like a winter burn bubbling over stone – the kind of sound that enchanted mortal men and otherwordly creatures alike. "Oh, kelpie," she said,

"Lachlan has offered her the world, and will continue to do so until the end of time."

Murdoch did not want to work out what that meant.

CHAPTER FIVE

Lachlan

It was freezing outside the Darrow house. Wet, stinging snow buffeted Lachlan and Sorcha; she wrapped her father's old coat a little tighter around herself.

"Did we really have to talk *out here,* Lachlan?" Sorcha complained, disapproval clear as day on her scrunched-up face. "The weather is horrible."

He pointed towards the parlour room window. "I do not want that damn horse listening to us as we speak, Clara."

"Do you have to talk about him like that? Lachlan, he came to me for *help.* He does not mean any –"

"If you say *harm,* Clara –"

"But all he wants to do is use Mr Buchanan's identity to stop our home from being destroyed!" Sorcha cut in, furious. "We all knew this was coming, and do not deny it. The entire reason my father betrothed me to Murdoch was to prevent this! If we sit around and do nothing then the man's colleagues – Grey and

29

MacKinnon and whoever else – will take everything away! They will come for my land and the loch and before you know it, Lachlan, they will come for the forest. So do not say we cannot help the kelpie."

Lachlan was taken aback; he had not seen a fire in Sorcha's eyes like this for months and months. For her to have *shouted* at him about the matter meant she truly had been worried about it for a long time. *She never talked to me about her concerns for the land. Why would she not confide in me?*

But the answer was right there, in front of him: she assumed Lachlan would not do what she had known in her heart had to be done over the past two years.

The kelpie needed its bridle back.

Lachlan punched the stone wall of Sorcha's house, then immediately regretted it. He hated demonstrating such physical acts of violence and frustration in front of *anyone,* let alone Sorcha. And now his hand throbbed.

He gritted his teeth against what he had to say next. "Fine," he muttered, without looking at Sorcha. "Fine. But there will be conditions, you hear me? You cannot simply –"

Lachlan's words were cut off by Sorcha flinging her arms around him. She was already cold and wet from the snow, but he did not care; he returned the embrace eagerly, lifting her off her feet in the process.

"Thank you," Sorcha said, voice sincere and affectionate. "Thank you, Lachlan. I knew you would not be foolish on this matter." When he finally placed her back on the ground she smiled and tucked a lock of flyaway hair behind an ear. "Now, can we *please* go back inside? I cannot feel my fingers."

He let out an exaggerated sigh. "If we must."

"We must."

It was with begrudging reluctance that Lachlan trudged back through to the parlour room, Sorcha not far behind him once she had removed her boots and her father's coat. She rushed over to the fire, crying out in happiness when the heat from the flames began to warm her hands up.

Murdoch watched her with such fondness that Lachlan almost picked up William Darrow's nearby silver letter opener and drove it through the kelpie's heart. But he resisted, though Ailith's keen eyes caught the subconscious flick of his wrist towards the potentially deadly weapon.

"Going by the look on your face," she said, "you have decided to relent to the kelpie's request."

"It seems we have no other choice, if we mean to protect our home," Lachlan replied, though it pained him to admit it.

Murdoch turned his gaze from Sorcha to Lachlan, eyes sharp with suspicion. "There are conditions, I am assuming?"

"Of course there are, you murderous, water-dwelling –"

"*Lachlan.*"

Both Sorcha and Ailith had spoken his name in identical warning tones. They glanced at each other, smiling softly; this was not the first time both of them had felt the need to chastise him in this manner. *You find a paramour and your queen becomes her best friend. Though it's only one more reason for Sorcha to join the Seelie Court.*

Murdoch watched the minute interaction between the two women with an expression that suggested he had come to the same conclusion as Lachlan had – that despite her growing responsibilities as an adult, Sorcha had been given more and more reasons to abandon her human life altogether over the past two years. Once she secured the Darrow land for good that would only be another point in the faerie realm's favour. Eventually, Lachlan hoped, she would give in and accept his offer to live in the Seelie Court – forever, if he had his way.

He relished that the kelpie clearly did not like that idea one bit.

Murdoch's voice was tightly controlled as he asked, "So what are the conditions?"

"Clara – Sorcha – will go with you to London, as Murdoch Buchanan's bride-to-be," Lachlan said, detesting the idea with every fibre of his being. "She will have complete control over your bridle. Where is it, Clara?"

Wordlessly she vacated the parlour room to retrieve it. Lachlan wondered where she kept it, for he had forced himself never to ask. If he knew then he would be tempted to destroy it, laws of ownership be damned. Instead, Lachlan contented himself with glaring at the kelpie, who bristled beneath the blanket Sorcha had given him to dry off. He looked frustratingly pitiable – the kind of pitiable that Sorcha would take it upon herself to address.

It was how she had come to help Lachlan break his fox curse, after all.

When Sorcha returned she had the kelpie's intricate silver bridle clutched protectively to her chest. Murdoch's entire being seemed to brighten simply by being in the same room as it.

Lachlan held out a hand. With noticeable hesitance Sorcha allowed him to touch the bridle; he did not wish to dwell upon that hesitance. "If you are ever further than a mile from Sorcha outside of London's borders," he began, "or if you try to take her anywhere she does not wish to go, you will lose your human form and all your powers. Take it or leave it, kelpie."

"I will take it, of course," Murdoch said. His jaw clenched as Lachlan wove his words into the bridle. Out of the corner of his eye Lachlan spied Ailith, poised and ready to defend him if Murdoch decided to use his temporary defencelessness to strike him down.

When Lachlan was done he let go of the bridle as if it had burned him, though in truth it was because he could not bear to touch it. It brought back too many memories of drowned faeries, and blood drenching the Seelie coronation plinth, and the kelpie telling him that he would not let Sorcha go.

"It is done," he muttered. Sorcha laid the bridle down on her armchair by the fire before returning to Lachlan's side to thank him. Clearly she intended to give it to Murdoch privately, which was an idea Lachlan did not relish. The two of them would be alone for days and potentially weeks on end, from the second Lachlan and Ailith walked out of the Darrow house until the moment Sorcha and Murdoch returned from London.

Lachlan did not want to leave without letting the kelpie know exactly what Sorcha was to him. "Do not make me regret helping you more than I already have," he warned the beast. "And..."

He wrapped an arm around Sorcha's waist and pulled her against him, hungrily kissing her as if it were the last time he might ever get to do so. For one awful moment she flinched, and Lachlan thought she might push him away, but then the tension melted and Sorcha allowed the kiss to happen.

Lachlan wanted to push it further. He wanted to, but he resisted.

He had a feeling Sorcha would tell him to stop, and Lachlan did not want to hear her say as much.

"Be careful, Clara," he whispered against her lips, for nobody to hear but her. Sorcha nodded the smallest of nods in return. When he finally broke away from her he turned to face Murdoch, a ferocious grin plastered to his face.

Murdoch looked positively murderous, which had of course been Lachlan's desired outcome. "...touch a single hair on Clara's head, kelpie," he said, voice eerily sing-song as he threatened Murdoch, "and I will ensure you lose *your* head in return."

He and Ailith spirited themselves out of Sorcha Darrow's house before the creature could respond.

CHAPTER SIX

Sorcha

It was three hours past midnight and Sorcha could not sleep.

The storm from earlier in the evening had finally abated, leaving the night soft and eerily quiet. Sorcha pulled back the curtain from her window and watched the clouds blow away, leaving the sky crisp and perfectly clear. Stars shone brightly upon the ink-black canvas; she thought there was something sad about them. Lonely. Heartbreakingly beautiful.

She wanted to be beneath them.

Without another thought Sorcha pulled on her boots and rushed out of her bedroom, forcing herself not to look at the guest bedroom door as she passed it. After Lachlan and Ailith left earlier that evening Murdoch had quickly admitted to being exhausted and excused himself for the night. Sorcha hadn't wanted him to, of course, but in truth Murdoch had looked so terrible she didn't feel like she had the right to stand between him and a soft bed. But one thing had confused Sorcha.

Murdoch hadn't put on his bridle.

She had taken it from the parlour room and laid it upon the floor outside the guest bedroom, in the hopes that Murdoch would open the door and find it during the night. However, it was currently exactly where Sorcha had left it, which caused her to frown in concern. *He has three hours of Unseelie magic left to use,* she thought, throwing on her father's old coat before easing open the front door and creeping outside. *I will have to awaken him soon. That is, if he is actually asleep.*

Given the last time Murdoch had slept in the Darrow guest bedroom, Sorcha doubted it very much.

"I wonder if he will follow me outside," she murmured, the words escaping her lips as puffs of icy breath upon the night air. It was even colder now than it had been when Lachlan dragged Sorcha outside to speak to her in private.

Too cold for snow. Too cold for noise.

Sorcha crunched over frozen grass towards the Darrow stable; since she was outside she reasoned she should check on Galileo. She was worried his water had iced over, and that the blankets she had thrown over him would not keep him warm enough against the bitter winter cold.

When she was halfway across the garden Sorcha paused to look up at the night sky. It seemed fathomless to her eyes, holding secrets that she would never be privy to. Knowledge of people and places and planets well beyond the scope of her understanding. It made her feel distinctly alone.

Perhaps it is not the stars that are lonely, then, Sorcha thought somewhat wistfully, letting out a heavy sigh before continuing on to Galileo's stable. She knew she'd been teetering on the edge of unhappiness ever since her parents had moved to Glasgow. It had been the right choice for them - and Sorcha was grateful that her father trusted her enough with the family business that he could leave her to work alone - but Sorcha missed them greatly.

"If only there were more unattached people my age around here," Sorcha grumbled for only the stars to hear, "but even Gregor MacPherson is now married with a babe on the way. There is only me left."

Sorcha flinched when the iron lock of Galileo's stable bit at her skin. It had not been this cold in Darach for years; Sorcha only vaguely remembered one winter as bitter as this from her youth. The snow had arrived early that year, and Old Man MacPherson and the other farmers had suffered a loss to their crop yields due to the frost. It had been a hard time for everyone, so Sorcha's father hadn't taken any rent from the residents on his land that winter.

One of many reasons why we have little and less money now, Sorcha thought, *though I would have done the same thing in my father's position.*

It was to her relief that Galileo's water trough was safe from the sub-zero temperatures; the fabric Sorcha had padded the metal and wooden barrel with had done a more than a serviceable job at keeping the water from freezing over. Galileo pawed at the straw floor of his stall as he watched her approach him, whinnying softly in response to Sorcha stroking a hand down along his nose.

"Are you warm enough, my love?" she cooed at the

stallion, rubbing her face against his when Galileo leaned in against her. His brown eyes shone in the darkness between slow, long-lashed blinks. "If I could have you inside the house with me I would, you know. You are my closest friend."

"That is both heartwarming and unbearably sad, Miss Darrow."

Sorcha's breath caught in her throat. "I had a feeling you were not asleep," she said, not daring to turn around. "Though I was going to awaken you soon if you were. You need to put on your bridle."

"I was merely relishing my final few hours in a human form that did not rely upon a silver chain," Murdoch said. Sorcha glanced over her shoulder; the kelpie was leaning against the door frame, body outlined in pale, luminous silver from the almost-full moon behind him. Along with the billowy white shirt he was wearing, the shadows beneath his eyes and the gauntness of his cheeks he appeared almost a ghost.

"You should not delay putting your bridle back on for such a reason. You really do not look well, Mist- Murdoch," Sorcha said, correcting her knee-jerk reaction to fall back on formalities.

Murdoch chuckled. "You can call me by whichever name you prefer, though I'd rather you didn't follow in your faerie's footsteps and call me *horse*."

"He is not *my* faerie," she protested, turning back to tickle Galileo's neck when he *harrumphed* at being ignored.

"It certainly seemed as if he considered you his," Murdoch countered. He walked towards Sorcha and Galileo, footsteps echoing all around the stable as he did so. When he held out a hand the stallion nibbled his fingers. "Hello, Galileo. It has been a while."

Sorcha frowned at the man who was not a man. "If Galileo was Mr Buchanan's horse then why does he like you? Surely he must know that you are not –"

"He knows," Murdoch cut in, voice quiet. He smoothed his hand along Galileo's neck; Sorcha watched him do so with rapt eyes. "He knows that I am not the master he had. But I am his friend, and he mine. That I ate Murdoch Buchanan is ultimately of no consequence to Galileo. It is simply my nature to consume humans, as it is his nature to feast upon grass."

When Murdoch's hand grazed against Sorcha's she did not pull away, though his touch was icy and his words sent a chill running down her spine. Her stomach was full of nerves at the prospect of acting as a dead man's wife-to-be, too, which only served to further discomfort her. It had been easy to stand up and tell Lachlan that she would gladly travel down to London to help the kelpie save her home.

Doing it was another thing entirely.

She sighed. "Murdoch –"

"Won't you take a walk with me, Sorcha?" he asked. She turned to see a knowing look upon his face, as if he had correctly surmised what was troubling her. He inclined his head politely. "If you are not too cold, that is."

Wordlessly Sorcha accepted, giving Galileo one final pat before exiting and locking the stable behind them. It should have come as no surprise that Murdoch wound his way across the Darrow garden towards the loch, though Sorcha did not complain. It was where she had planned to go herself, after all.

"You are concerned about London," Murdoch said after a while. He was shivering slightly; the shirt and breeches Sorcha had found for him from her father's wardrobe were hardly enough to keep out the winter air.

She made a face. "You should have put on a coat."

"And you are deflecting."

"We should head back and get –"

Murdoch reached out and squeezed Sorcha's wrist. Her cheeks began to burn at his touch, though she passed it off as a reaction to the cold. "I will be fine," he said. "I am not human, and this vessel the Unseelie gave me is near spent, anyway. Once I put on my bridle I will be in good health once more."

Sorcha did not like the idea of Murdoch's current form dying before her very eyes at all, though it was clear the kelpie did not care, so eventually she let go of her concern. "Yes," she sighed, taking several long strides towards Loch Lomond across slippery, ice-encrusted grass. "I am worried about London. Are you not, Murdoch?"

His ears pricked at Sorcha's use of the name. When they reached the shore along the water's edge he kicked at the sand, sending it flying several feet in front of him. "Of course I am," he admitted. "It is not often I find myself venturing out of Scotland – not least to live as a human in the busiest city in Britain."

"Do you...do you know what we need to do when we get there?"

Murdoch nodded. He pointed to his temple. "Mister Buchanan's memories are invaluable. I should have no problem acting as the man himself whilst we are in London."

Sorcha's stomach lurched once more. She knelt by the loch, holding a shaking hand a mere inch above its surface. She had not touched it in two years, for fear of what she would – or wouldn't – find in the water upon making contact. But now the kelpie was beside her, carelessly skimming stones across the very loch that was his home.

Why am I so nervous? Sorcha worried. *I was not so bad back in my house earlier this evening. What has changed?* She stole a glance at Murdoch through her wild, tangled hair. He was kneeling beside her now, and had stuck his hand into the freezing water without a moment's hesitation. His eyes were dark and vacant, like a mirror in a shadowy corridor.

Perhaps it was because of the frost, or the moonlight, or the proximity of the loch, or the Unseelie's magic, but even under the guise of a human Sorcha did not think the kelpie *looked* human. Not at all.

How did I ever think he was simply a man?

"You truly do have an unfortunate habit of staring, Miss Darrow," Murdoch said without tearing his eyes away from the loch. "I thought your parents raised you to have better manners than this."

Sorcha bristled, then stood up with her hands curled into fists at her side. "I –"

"I jest," Murdoch laughed, thoroughly amused. He removed his hand from the loch and dried it upon his breeches. "I forgot how easy it is to burrow under your skin, Sorcha."

When Sorcha's insides twisted this time it was not

entirely uncomfortable. She scratched behind her ear and looked away. "That is not very kind of you, you know," she mumbled, but Murdoch merely laughed again.

"Says the woman who once fled out of her bedroom window to avoid having to speak to me when I had not done anything wrong."

"You ate the man you were masquerading as!"

"I suppose I did. Should we head back inside?"

Sorcha nodded, thinking as they headed back towards her house that it should not have been so easy for her to talk about a man's horrific death as if it were merely a piece of casual, passing conversation. But the kelpie had been correct back in the stable – it was in his nature to devour humans. Sorcha could not blame him for eating Mr Buchanan, no more than she could blame the men who hunted deer in the forest for venison.

The two of them walked in companionable silence across the garden, the only sound the soft lapping of the loch upon the shore, when Murdoch slipped on the icy grass with a yell of surprise, and grabbed onto Sorcha's arm before he could stop himself.

"Careful!" she exclaimed, heart hammering in her chest as she just barely kept herself upright. Murdoch had fallen down on one knee, so Sorcha held out a hand to help him back up. A smile crossed her lips before she could stop herself. "Perhaps you should spend more time on your own two feet," she said, thinking back to the first time she had said such a thing to the kelpie before she knew he was anything but a man.

Murdoch's dark, fathomless eyes were perfect reflections of the starry night sky as he looked up at

Sorcha; she almost gasped at the sight of it. His fingers tightened around her hand, and he slowly got back up on his feet. "Perhaps I should," he agreed, "though if my balance got better then I would not have the pleasure of you saving me, Miss Darrow."

He is dangerous, Sorcha thought, stricken by the memory of being held by the kelpie in her tent two years ago. *He was dangerous then and he is even more dangerous now.*

She did not have it in her to be scared of that danger anymore.

"Come," Sorcha mumbled, tearing her hand away from Murdoch's before her mind raced even further down memory lane. "You should get back inside and put on your bridle. You look like death."

"I feel like it, too."

Sorcha chuckled softly. "And that just won't do. We need to be in the best of health for travelling down to London. The journey will take us days."

"...it may not be as long as you think."

She cocked her head to one side, regarding Murdoch suspiciously as he closed the front door behind them and made for the guest bedroom. He picked up his bridle from the floor when he reached it, an unreadable expression on his face that hid everything he was thinking about.

"What do you mean by that?" she asked, continuing down the corridor until she reached her own bedroom door. Something told her that she should give the kelpie his privacy when putting on his bridle, though Sorcha did not know why. She was hardly an expert on magical creature etiquette, after all.

But Murdoch did not answer her question. He merely smirked.

"Good night, Sorcha Darrow," he said, closing the guest bedroom door before Sorcha had an opportunity to press him further on the matter.

When she lay back in bed it came as absolutely no surprise that her mind was racing far too wildly to fall asleep. *Morning cannot come quickly enough,* Sorcha thought, staring at her door as if she could see right through it to Murdoch's bedroom.

With a sigh she rolled over and forced herself to close her eyes. "What a strange day this has been," she whispered, simply to acknowledge that the events of the day had indeed happened.

Sorcha knew in her heart that the following days were only going to get stranger.

CHAPTER SEVEN

Sorcha

By the time Sorcha had washed, dressed, combed her hair and laced on her boots Murdoch was already out in the stable preparing Galileo for the long ride to London. But when she spied him walking the stallion towards Old Man MacPherson's farm Sorcha grew confused and concerned.

Just what is going on? she wondered, trying her best to settle her nerves by preparing breakfast for herself and Murdoch. Sorcha still had to pack for the trip but in truth she had no idea what to bring. She certainly had no clothes that were expensive enough to wear surrounded by the upper classes of London gentry. *Murdoch will know what to pack,* she reassured herself. *Or, at least, Mister Buchanan will.*

It was getting very confusing for Sorcha, constantly thinking of the kelpie and the man as different people. Perhaps she was better combining the two for the sake of her act as his bride-to-be...as well as her sanity.

"Something smells wonderful," Murdoch called out when he returned to the house fifteen minutes later. He breathed in deeply through his nose, smiling broadly for Sorcha when she turned from the cooking fire to say good morning.

"There's little point in leaving any sausages or eggs in the house when we do not know when we'll be back," she said, emptying the overfull contents of a large cast iron pan onto two plates. She frowned at Murdoch. "Why did you take Galileo over to the MacPherson farm?"

He avoided her gaze, evading answering the question by spearing a sausage off his plate and consuming the entire thing whole. With a sigh of impatience Sorcha dug into her own breakfast. *I suppose I'll find out exactly how we're travelling in due time,* she thought, inspecting Murdoch with careful eyes as he devoured every morsel of food on his plate.

Murdoch looked a thousand times better than he had done the night before. Gone were the shadows beneath his eyes, the skull-like hollowness of his cheeks, the hunched posture of someone trying hard not to vomit, and the sickly pallor of his skin. He had returned to being just as handsome, broad-shouldered and strong as Sorcha remembered the man being two years ago, even in her father's ill-fitting clothes. Around Murdoch's neck the delicate silver chain of his bridle was just barely visible beneath the collar of his borrowed shirt.

But one thing remained changed from two years ago.

"Why is your hair longer than it was when I met you?" Sorcha asked, curiosity getting the better of her as she took both of their empty plates over to the wash basin. "Surely Mr Buchanan's form does not need to age."

Murdoch ran a hand through his loose, shoulder-length curls and shrugged. "It is a reflection of how much time has passed for me. Of how things have changed."

"So *you* altered it? Deliberately?"

He nodded. "Do you mislike it, Sorcha?"

"No," she replied a little too quickly, taken entirely by surprise by the kelpie wanting her opinion on the matter. She blushed. "No," Sorcha said again, slowly this time. "I like it. Though it may get meddlesome as we travel down to London through all this bad weather we've been having. Heaven knows I wish I could simply chop off all of my –"

"Do not even dare suggesting cutting off your hair," Murdoch warned. "It is beautiful."

She scoffed, then blew an errant lock of hair out of her face. "It is always a mess," Sorcha complained. "I'm no good at making it look nice the way my mother does. I wonder how I'll ever manage to pass myself off as a *lady* in London. I don't even know what to pack! And –"

"Ah, so that was what you were fussing over for so long in your bedroom," Murdoch said, understanding dawning on his face as he smiled. He stood up from the kitchen table, waving for Sorcha to join him in the hallway. When he removed her father's old coat from a hook on the wall and passed it over to her she hesitated before putting it on.

"You do not need to pack anything," he said. "We can buy everything we need in London." He fished through a small bureau that sat beneath the hallway mirror until he found a length of thin rope. Murdoch

47

grinned at it. "Perfect," he murmured, scraping back his hair from his face before using the rope to tie it back. Sorcha had to admit she liked the look of him with his hair this way, though she resisted saying as much out loud.

She used her reflection in the mirror to braid back her own unruly hair, spinning it into a knot at the base of her neck before asking, "Are we really not taking Galileo to London?"

Murdoch caught hold of Sorcha's gaze in the mirror. His shoulders straightened, and he coughed softly. "There are...far faster ways to travel than by road, especially when the weather is so disagreeable." He turned towards the front door and unlocked it, letting a burst of bitter air through that stung Sorcha's cheeks. His eyes narrowed against the brightness of the frost covering the Darrow garden. "The sooner we set out, the sooner we will arrive at our destination."

Sorcha made to follow Murdoch to the door, but a glint in the mirror gave her pause. She peered at it, believing it to be the sun shining through and hitting the glass before realising that said sun was obscured by thick, white clouds. The glimmer remained even when she looked at the mirror from a different angle, cocking her head so far to the side that her ear brushed against her shoulder.

Murdoch laughed at her from the porch. "What on earth are you doing, Sorcha?"

"Nothing," she murmured softly. When Sorcha focused on the mirror again the glint was gone. She blinked a few times, confused, then decided she was clearly very tired and was therefore seeing things. *It will be a long time before I reach a bed,* Sorcha thought, glancing wistfully at her bedroom door. *But it is my own fault I could not sleep.*

When Murdoch led Sorcha through the dull, freezing morning towards Loch Lomond she grew ever more uncertain. "Just what are we doing here?" she demanded, when Murdoch stopped precisely where the water lapped against the shore.

He rolled his left shoulder until it cracked, staring out across the loch instead of answering Sorcha's question. Then he tugged the silver chain of his bridle an inch or two away from his neck so she could see it clearly, glittering like diamonds in the winter air. Sorcha held out a hand towards it before she could stop herself.

"You now hold dominion over my powers, Miss Darrow," Murdoch said, tone careful and serious. "I have not been in this position before. I never thought I would be able to bear it. But if the person in control of me is *you*, then..." He smiled. "I think I can handle it. And since you are now connected to the bridle..."

Sorcha was just barely beginning to grasp at what Murdoch was insinuating when his form began to ripple and warp. She had seen him transform into his true self only once, in the memory of a nightmare in the middle of the Seelie Court. Now, in the broad light of day outside her house, the way the very lines of his body dissolved and changed in front of Sorcha's eyes seemed more a hallucination than anything real, just like the glimmer in the hallway mirror.

Between the space of one blink and the next Murdoch Buchanan was gone, replaced with an enormous, hulking, pitch-black horse. Tiny bones and strands of murky green weed were knotted into the kelpie's long, flowing mane, and when he opened his mouth two rows of sharp, deadly teeth were revealed. The chain around his neck had become a silver and blackened leather bridle once more.

When Murdoch-the-kelpie spoke he startled Sorcha so badly she tripped. "Get on," he said, bending low on his front legs for her to climb onto his back.

"I can't – Murdoch, how do we get from here to London like this?" she asked, at a loss for anything else to say. She was transfixed by the form of the enormous creature kneeling before her.

His tail twitched. "Through the water, of course."

"But I can't breathe under water! And Loch Lomond is not in any way connected to –"

"Just get on, and you will see," Murdoch said. He laughed at the look on Sorcha's face, though it sounded distinctly inhuman. She crept towards him on unsteady legs, holding an outstretched hand an inch or two away from his neck before stopping.

Sorcha knew she was trembling. "I am afraid," she admitted, for there was no use in lying to the kelpie. He turned his head and knocked against Sorcha's cheek with his nose; the air he huffed out was warm and reassuring on her skin.

Murdoch kept one large, impossibly dark eye on Sorcha's face. "To be afraid of the unknown is natural," he said. "But I will not let any harm come to you. You will be safe. I swear it."

Her hand was still trembling when Sorcha ran it through the kelpie's mane, but she ignored it. Taking a deep breath she hitched herself onto the creature's back, swinging a leg over and wobbling unsteadily as Murdoch lifted himself onto all four of his gargantuan hooves.

Now that he was standing at his full height Sorcha realised just how much taller he was than a real horse.

I am riding a giant, she thought. *An otherworldly, incomprehensible giant.*

"Do not let me fall," she said, smoothing her hands against the glossy hair of Murdoch's neck before entwining her fingers through his mane for dear life.

Murdoch chuckled his inhuman chuckle once more, then took a few steps into the loch. "I won't," he replied, and then – against all logic or sense – dove straight into the loch and dissolved into the water, taking Sorcha with him.

Sorcha had always thought that if she found herself riding a kelpie it would be to her doom. That was what all the stories warned people about, after all.

She never imagined she would use such a creature to travel down to London.

CHAPTER EIGHT

Murdoch

Murdoch had never felt so free. Despite the fact a human had complete control over his powers, and that same human was currently riding on his back, he felt ecstatic. Wild. Invincible.

If he'd ever doubted whether he still had feelings for Sorcha Darrow after two years banished to the bottom of Loch Lomond, he most certainly didn't now. Everything that had happened over the span of the last twenty-four hours was enough to tell him that he was still hopelessly, painfully in love with her.

Particularly the way she clung to his ghostly, ever-changing form as he barrelled down to London through every body of water he could find.

I am not scared, I am not scared, I am not –

"I can hear you, remember."

Sorcha flinched against Murdoch's back, and he laughed. "I told you not to be frightened," he said, as they left Loch Lomond behind to pass through the Firth of Clyde. Murdoch planned to follow the Firth into the Irish Sea, then head back inland via the River Mersey. Then it was a case of hopping from river to river, lake to lake, and stream to stream until they reached London.

Murdoch had not travelled in such a way over a distance as long as this for at least three human generations. After spending two long years imprisoned in his own home he found the space around him incredibly liberating. And he was getting to show Sorcha Darrow how exactly he could move from place to place so quickly, too, thus teaching her more about him.

He never wanted the journey to end.

Though Murdoch was melting into each body of water he passed through, making use of currents to travel as quickly as possible, he was still keenly aware of Sorcha's arms wrapped around his neck and her thighs squeezing against his back. Her face was buried in his mane; whenever he made a sharp turn she cried out a mouthful of bubbles and buried herself even deeper into his hair.

How can I breathe? she thought at him. *How am I alive? How are we travelling so fast?*

"Because you can wield my bridle," Murdoch said, veering out of the way of a large shoal of cod when they appeared on his left. "It is difficult to explain. But so long as you are touching me you will not drown."

Sorcha's mind was silent of all but the barest thought for a long time after that, but eventually her grip began to loosen just a little and Murdoch felt her relax. *Can you always move this fast?* she asked him.

He nodded. "Only if I merge with the water, though. To keep a solid form I must move far more slowly."

Do other kelpies not mind when you swim through their homes?

"We are only passing through, so it is acceptable. If I were to linger and challenge them then they would not be so hospitable."

Sorcha mulled over this for a few moments; Murdoch thoroughly enjoyed listening into her thought process. He came to quickly realise that, for every question she vocalised, another dozen or so went unsaid. Murdoch had always thought Sorcha spoke her mind without consequence – just as she acted without consequence – but now he wasn't so sure.

There was so much he did not know about the woman currently wondering how on earth the two of them were going to avoid suspicion upon arriving in London, dripping wet and without any luggage.

"Murdoch Buchanan's townhouse lies close to the Thames," he explained for Sorcha's benefit. "It will be dark when we arrive, so it is unlikely anybody will see us appear from the water. It is but a minute or two's walk to the front door."

Sorcha lifted her head from Murdoch's neck as if she meant to speak out loud. *Won't the house be locked?* she asked. *And in disrepair? Mister Buchanan has not been back for two years.*

"The house has been kept in good condition by his housekeeper, Mrs Ferguson," Murdoch replied. He flinched at the drop in water temperature when they moved into the Irish Sea from the Firth of Clyde. "I have kept in contact with her all this time."

How?

"There is a selkie who lives in London who has

been writing letters on Murdoch's behalf and passing them over to her," he said. "Last night I sent word to the selkie to inform Mrs Ferguson of our imminent arrival, so the house should be ready for us by the time we reach it."

How did you send word down? Sorcha asked. *You never –*

"Remember when I dipped my hand in the loch? I called for a messenger to pass along my orders to another messenger in the Firth of Clyde, and so on and so forth."

...oh.

Murdoch felt a pang of sympathy for Sorcha. He was springing a lot of information on her at once in his excitement and eagerness for her to understand how the life of a kelpie worked. How *his* life worked. It was not fair of him to do so.

"You do not need to think about these things so much if you cannot wrap your head around them just now," Murdoch said after a moment of silence. "The magic of kelpies is –"

"I have spent two years as a friend to the Seelie Court," Sorcha said aloud, the words escaping her mouth as a riot of bubbles. "I might not understand magic the way I would if I possessed it, but it does not trouble me. I simply wish..." Her sentence trailed off to nothing.

"Sorcha?"

She sighed. *I wish I had known all of this about you before now.*

Murdoch's heart stung; his entire body rippled beneath Sorcha's. "I would have told you," he said, very quietly, "had you touched the loch even once over the last two years."

I thought you might drag me down to die for how I betrayed you, Sorcha admitted. *Or worse, ignore me.*

"You believe me ignoring you is worse than killing you?"

Yes.

"You are so strange."

Says the kelpie to the human.

Neither of them spoke to each other for a while after that, Sorcha's mind growing distant as she fell prey to drowsiness and Murdoch concentrating on hopping from river to lake and stream until he finally caught the murky scent of the Thames. By the time he crashed through the dark surface of the river to land upon the paved street beside it Sorcha had almost fallen asleep; Murdoch's change back to a human abruptly brought her back to consciousness.

"We are – we are here?" she spluttered, coughing and shivering as she did so. She stared at Murdoch with wide eyes. "The water did not feel so cold when we were in it, but the air is freezing!"

Murdoch smiled sympathetically, wrapping an arm around Sorcha's shoulders before leading her on shaking legs along the abandoned promenade in the direction of Mr Buchanan's townhouse. It was bizarre, to know exactly where he was going based on someone else's memories masquerading as his own, though it was not the first time Murdoch had taken on the guise of a man he had consumed. It was merely the longest time he had done so, and the most serious.

By the time he reached a grand, handsomely-carved

front door Murdoch had to admit he was nervous. But he couldn't be nervous – not when Sorcha was relying on him to know what he was doing. *Just be Murdoch Buchanan,* he thought. *You did it before. You can do it again.*

But that meant not being himself, and Murdoch did not like that at all. It had been hard enough to blend the man's personality with his own back when he had first introduced himself to Sorcha Darrow; even harder when he had travelled around the loch with her. Now Murdoch would have to ensure none of his own self slipped through the cracks whilst he was in London, for if Grey and MacKinnon or any of Mr Buchanan's other associates suspected something was awry then his and Sorcha's attempts to save their home would be ruined.

Feeling in a distinctly worse mood than he had been but a moment ago, Murdoch rang the bell that hung over the door and waited patiently for the sound of someone scurrying down the stairs to wrench it open. They were greeted by Mrs Ferguson, Mr Buchanan's housekeeper: a woman of slight stature, middling age and greying hair, whose blue eyes widened when she took in Murdoch and Sorcha's appearance.

"Mister Buchanan!" she exclaimed, ushering the two of them inside before closing the door behind them. "What ever happened to you? And you must be Miss Darrow! You are frozen half to death!"

Sorcha smiled somewhat rigidly, as if her face was truly made of ice. "It is a pleasure to meet you, Mrs Ferguson."

"We were caught in a bit of a flurry just outside the city," Murdoch lied in lieu of having to explain how exactly the two of them were soaked through. "I will admit that we certainly feel frozen half to death. Is the fire going in my bedroom?"

The servant nodded, following them up the stairs until they reached the main hallway of a house that was both familiar and alien to Murdoch's eyes. "The bath is ready," she said, "and I have prepared a platter of food in your room should you be hungry."

"Thank you, Mrs Ferguson," Murdoch replied, touching Sorcha gently on the shoulder to direct her towards Mr Buchanan's bedroom. "Miss Darrow and I are both exhausted, so that will be all for the evening. We shall talk in the morning."

Without another word the housekeeper retreated into what Murdoch knew was the kitchen. Sorcha began staring unabashedly at everything she saw, but Murdoch put an end to her gawking by gently pushing her into his bedroom.

"You take the bath," he said, shoulders slumping with relief the moment the heat from the fire Mrs Ferguson had lit in the hearth tickled his skin.

Sorcha shook her head. "I am...too tired," she yawned, stripping off her soaked and frozen clothing without so much as an ounce of modesty; Murdoch watched her in stunned silence for a long moment before turning from her in a panic. "I wish merely to heat up by the fire and crawl into bed. Don't you, Murdoch? Murdoch?"

"...ah, yes, I agree," he mumbled, pulling off his own clothes and throwing on the first voluminous shirt he could find in the wardrobe as quickly as he could. He filtered through the clothes inside until he located another, then flung it at Sorcha without looking at her. "This will have to do until tomorrow."

She laughed softly. "It will do after tomorrow, too. You know I am not fussy with my clothes."

Murdoch risked a glance behind him and was relieved to find that Sorcha had put on the shirt. It fell to the mid-point of her thighs and was so wide around the shoulder that it threatened to slip off her frame entirely, causing Murdoch to remember the one night in Sorcha's tent when he had slept with her curled against his chest.

An ache of longing twisted somewhere beneath his stomach.

But Murdoch could not act on his impulses; not when he was supposed to be someone else. For Sorcha was not *his* wife-to-be, and the entire engagement was a charade in the first place. No, Murdoch had to keep a respectful distance, at least whilst the two of them were in London.

He wished he had asked Mrs Ferguson to prepare the guest bedroom but Murdoch, in his excitement and distinct lack of human sense and sensibility, hadn't wanted to part from Sorcha for even a moment whilst they stayed together.

How he regretted that decision now.

Sorcha perched herself delicately on the bed, wincing as she ran her fingers through her hair to detangle it. She raised an eyebrow at Murdoch. "Are you going to stand by the fire all night, or are you coming to bed?" she asked, clearly oblivious to the thoughts currently tormenting Murdoch at that very moment.

He closed the distance between them and crept beneath the covers, careful to avoid looking at Sorcha as she collapsed against the pillow beside him with a contented cry. "Good night, Miss Darrow," Murdoch said, turning his back on her before he could do anything he might later regret.

"...good night, *Mister Buchanan*," Sorcha replied, the amused tone to her voice only stinging Murdoch further as she settled herself down to sleep. Despite everything that had happened since he had shown up at her door – the electric current between them, the fact Sorcha had not let anyone take his bridle away from her, the ease with which they had spoken to each other – Murdoch knew he had to be careful. He could not be himself right now.

He had to be Mr Buchanan.

And yet, regardless of the circumstances, sharing a room with Sorcha Darrow and not being able to touch her was a torment even worse for Murdoch than losing his powers to the Seelie King.

CHAPTER NINE

Lachlan

Lachlan's eyes were wide open, though he knew the sun was already as high in the sky as it would go. He should have been fast asleep. He *should* have, but thoughts of Sorcha in London with the kelpie were haunting him. They had been gone for but two days. Two.

Lachlan had no idea how he was supposed to cope with her being alone with the creature for weeks.

"Sleep, Lachlan," Ailith murmured without opening her eyes, rolling over to place a placating hand on his bare chest. But Lachlan slid away from it, creeping out of bed and tossing on a deep green, spider-silk robe that fell in large swathes of fabric to the floor. Though he was loathe to leave the warmth the dying embers in the massive hearth provided, Lachlan could stand to stay still even less.

And so, bracing himself against the chill of the palace corridors, Lachlan eased the large, carved doors of his chambers open on silent hinges. He spared a final glance at the sleeping figure of his queen, whose pale hair was perfectly dishevelled across several pillows and glimmered in the low light of the room like white gold. He smiled at her, then carefully closed the doors behind him and stalked aimlessly away.

Ailith would say I was over-reacting if I told her how I felt, Lachlan thought. *She would tell me that Sorcha can handle herself. That she has full control over the kelpie's powers. Perhaps I am over-reacting. But I cannot help it, all things considered.*

The sconces along the smooth, curved walls of the palace were barely lit with flickering flames, and all windows were covered from the dull noonday sun; most everyone was asleep save for a sparse scattering of guards. They bowed their heads respectfully when then realised their king was passing them by. Even in darkness the corridors shone faintly gold, illuminating Lachlan's skin as if from within.

He remembered the first time he had stolen away through the palace with Sorcha in tow. She had lulled the kelpie to sleep in Lachlan's bedroom – had sung him a song in a voice so soft and gentle Lachlan had almost bowled down the door to interrupt it. Even now, two years later, he hated that Sorcha had sung for anyone but him.

She might sing for the kelpie again, Lachlan's brain chimed in unhelpfully. He bit at his lip and shook his long hair out of his face, beyond irritated. Lachlan wished it was acceptable for him to travel down to London himself to keep watch over her, but he knew it was impossible. Until the winter solstice revel he could not justify leaving the Seelie Court – not even for Sorcha.

62

Lachlan found himself outside the heavy iron door that protected his favourite place in the entire palace from lesser fae. The power of the metal thrummed in the air, stinging Lachlan's hands even though he was not quite touching it, but with a singular thought the door swung open and granted him entrance.

The room was dark, as usual, but Lachan's keen eyes quickly adjusted until he could pick out every phosphorescent mushroom, coloured gemstone and pit of pillows and blankets that punctuated the floor. A shallow burn snaked its way across the ages-worn stone, bubbling into the room from some hidden, underground spring and leaving via an invisible crack in a wall into the forest.

Lachlan watched his reflection in the crystalline water for a few moments, distressed to see a scowl curling his lips back from his teeth. He quickly wiped it from his face. It was a remnant of his time as a fox, he knew – something that the kelpie had made even worse by stabbing Lachlan whilst he had been cursed. Sometimes Lachlan woke up unable to speak, or found himself longing to leap into a pile of fallen leaves to rub his non-existent fur across them. He craved raw pheasant and rabbit on occasion, too, which wouldn't have been so odd if he didn't also desire to catch the birds with his own jaws.

If the foreign wizard Julian hadn't healed Lachlan's stab wound he would still be a fox. All these tics served as reminders of how close he had been to losing himself forever.

"Clara," he murmured at his reflection, before breaking the surface with his hand in order to splash the bracing water of the burn over his face. He wished dearly to see her; to braid her hair and slip her dress from her shoulders and whisper promises of forever into her ear. He wanted all the things he currently could not have.

If only I could reach her dreams, Lachlan thought longingly, collapsing into the pit of pillows where they had first lain together in real life. If he closed his eyes Lachlan could almost imagine the smell of Sorcha from that heady, dangerous night. Bluebells and lilac. Dirt beneath her fingernails and sweat on her skin. The hint of the loch, ever-present in her hair.

"I want her," he moaned, grasping onto a red-and-gold cushion as if it were Sorcha herself. And then Lachlan had an idea. His powers had grown since he'd first ascended the throne of the Seelie king. Just because he'd never tried to enter a mortal's dreams from as far away as London before did not mean he *couldn't* do it.

A small smile curled his lips at the thought. If he could do it – if he could reach Sorcha across hundreds and hundreds of miles – then it would not matter that Lachlan could not currently leave the faerie realm.

He couldn't wait to see the look on her face when she realised that she was not imagining Lachlan inside her head, just like the first time he had invaded the girl's dreams. Sorcha would be happy about it. More than happy, Lachlan knew. They had a relationship that nobody else understood, least of all the kelpie.

"She is mine, horse," Lachlan said, the promise of seeing Sorcha finally lulling him into a slow, contented sleep.

CHAPTER TEN

Murdoch

It was simultaneously awkward, pleasing and incredibly frustrating for Murdoch to wake up with Sorcha beside him for the third morning in a row. Awkward, because they were still somewhat surprised to see the other upon first waking up. Pleasing, because Murdoch could think of nothing better than watching Sorcha struggle between curling back beneath the covers to sleep for longer and deciding to stay awake. Incredibly frustrating, because there was nothing worse than resisting the urge to touch Sorcha when she, still half-asleep, rolled right into Murdoch's arms and slid her bare legs between his own.

It was a delicious torture.

They had spent their first full day in London largely unconscious, so exhausted from the previous twenty-four hours that their bodies demanded an exorbitant amount of rest to make up for it.

On the second day, Murdoch arranged a messenger

to send word to Grey and MacKinnon that Mr Buchanan had returned to London and wished to meet as soon as was possible, as well as organised the man's personal office and finances. Sorcha had contented herself with exploring the house, talking to Mrs Ferguson and memorising maps of London.

If she noticed the distance Murdoch had put between them she did not make it apparent.

On the third morning the two of them were woken by Mrs Ferguson, informing Murdoch that Grey and MacKinnon wished for him to come to their office that very day. Sorcha complained profusely when Murdoch rose from bed and ripped open the curtains, shining morning sunshine through the window straight onto her face. It was a beautiful day, for which Murdoch was grateful; he did not have it in him to put up with sleet and snow.

"Am I coming with you?" Sorcha grumbled, huddled beneath the covers with an expression that very much implied she did not wish to move from the bed ever again.

Murdoch shook his head, then pulled a white shirt over his hair. "No; I imagine the company will invite you to some kind of luncheon or dinner party once I have spoken to them," he said. He stumbled slightly as he pulled on a pair of deep, wine-coloured trousers that he'd taken a fancy to from Mr Buchanan's wardrobe. "Though, with any luck, we can convince them to leave Loch Lomond alone and head back home before we have to do much socialising."

"I would not mind socialising."

He raised an eyebrow in Sorcha's direction. "*I am scared of strangers. Particularly those from London. A* fiery, opinionated lass once told me that."

Sorcha rolled onto her back, tilting her head to watch Murdoch upside-down. She snickered. "You have a good memory. But I am here to be Mr Buchanan's wife-to-be, am I not? And I have never been to London before. It would be a waste not to look around and be a tourist. Heaven knows I've had to deal with my fair share of them back home; it's about time I get to be one myself!"

"I suppose that is fair." Murdoch considered her answer as he slipped on a tailcoat that matched his trousers and a pair of knee-high, black leather boots. A tall, round hat hung innocuously from a hook by a full-length mirror; Murdoch put it on and fussed around with his curly locks of hair.

Sorcha let out a low whistle. "Those clothes look absurdly good on you, Murdoch," she said. Through the reflection in the mirror he noticed a flush had spread across her cheeks; it spelled trouble for his heart rate.

He coughed softly, picking up a soft pair of white, doe-skin gloves and a black overcoat as he made his way to the door. "It appears our Mr Buchanan has excellent taste," he murmured. He turned to face the bed. "Speaking of clothes, Mrs Ferguson is going to accompany you shopping today, if you are up to it."

"I suppose I could be convinced to leave this bed," Sorcha drawled, a lazy grin spreading across her face as she stretched her arms across a silken, brocade coverlet. Her shirt was no longer covering her legs at all; Murdoch had to remind himself to stop openly staring at her in such a state of undress.

She is making my life impossible.

Murdoch coughed once more. "I...should be off, then," he said, thrusting open the bedroom door and darting out of the house before Sorcha or even Mrs Ferguson had an opportunity to say goodbye.

*

"Well if it isn't our long, lost Mr Buchanan!"

Murdoch plastered a genial smile to his face as he greeted a room full of people he largely recognised. The oldest gentleman in the room, Howard Grey, was portly, grey-haired and nearly sixty years old. He grinned as he shook Murdoch's hand. His business partner, Gregory MacKinnon, was a few years younger and several pounds lighter than him, with hair that was still black as pitch. His smile was a little tight as he took his turn in shaking Murdoch's hand.

There were three other men whom Murdoch recognised sitting at the large, polished mahogany table which took up much of the room: the board's treasurer, James Campbell; their secretary, William Wright, and a junior partner to the firm, Francis Smith. But there was one final person Murdoch had not met before sitting at the table, who was perhaps around thirty years old. Going by his similar appearance to Gregory MacKinnon, Murdoch could only assume the man was his son.

"Mister Buchanan, this is my son Donald," Gregory said, confirming Murdoch's assumption as he sat down beside him.

"Don," his son corrected, rolling his eyes at the older man. "Calling me Mr MacKinnon would be confusing with my father around, and I rather dislike *Donald*. It sounds like a farmer's name."

Murdoch could say nothing to the contrary, for he

had known several farmers called Donald over the past few centuries. He had even eaten a few of them.

"It is a pleasure to meet you," Murdoch said politely. When Howard handed him a crystalline glass full of whisky Murdoch had no choice but to accept it, though it was barely noon – going by Mr Buchanan's memories the man never turned down a drink. The fact that they'd chosen *whisky* to drink was clearly a jibe made at Murdoch's expense because he'd lived in Scotland for the past two years; all of his previous memories pointed to the board members of Grey and MacKinnon favouring port.

"We brought him in to take over most of your duties in your absence," Gregory said, indicating towards Don, "though Norman over at the bank was not happy to lose him."

Ah, that explains why he is tense with me, Murdoch realised. *He does not want his son to give up his position within the business. Well, once I've dealt with the matter of Sorcha's land then he can have it.*

"So, Murdoch," Howard said, forgoing formalities now that everyone was sitting down and sipping upon amber whisky, "how goes it up in Scotland? Must have been something wonderful there to keep you from London for so long. Or some*one*, rather."

Murdoch did not have to fake his reaction to the man's question. The top of his ears began to burn merely thinking of Sorcha, and an abashed smile flashed across his face before he could contain it. Howard laughed at his response.

"She is that lovely? Why, we must meet the lass if she is fair enough to entrap our dear Murdoch Buchanan."

"Miss Darrow has travelled down with me to London," Murdoch said, straightening his back as he spoke. It was time to get down to business. "She has never been out of Scotland before, and was curious to meet the people I work with."

Gregory clapped his hands together. "Then so she shall! Although – and permit me for being intrusive – why have you not married Miss Darrow yet? We expected you to own the land long before now, Mr Buchanan."

"She wished to take things slowly. Considering the other option was to run back to London, thoroughly rejected, I had no choice but to oblige her request."

"A careful woman," Gregory observed. "Which is no surprise, considering how resistant her father was to anyone buying the land when it was in his name." He narrowed his eyes at Murdoch. "Does she have any idea what you plan to do with the land once it is signed over to you?"

"Considering I am unsure about what exactly the plans *are,* no," Murdoch admitted. He threw back the rest of the whisky in his glass and turned to Howard. He wasn't as sly as Gregory; he was more likely to get the truth out of him. "I have heard rumour of your intention to fill in the shallowest shores along the southern bank of Loch Lomond," he said. "Is this true?"

Howard shrugged. "We were growing impatient with your extended, love-struck stay with your betrothed, Murdoch. The Darrows do not own every stretch of the southern shore. If we turn those areas into holiday and hunting accommodation then we can work around the Darrow land until, eventually, the lass will have us on all sides forcing her to sell. It is not the first time we have used such a tactic."

"No," Murdoch said, working hard to keep his voice level, "but it is the first time you have done it behind the back of one of your own."

"Well now that you're here we won't have to resort to such disreputable tactics," Howard said, patting Murdoch amiably on the back. "Have you considered marrying Miss Darrow whilst in London? We are hosting a winter ball on the twenty-first. It would make everything far easier if she signed all of the property paperwork down here."

Murdoch hesitated. "The twenty-first is almost three weeks away," he said. "I did not intend to –"

"Surely you do not plan to move up to Scotland permanently, Mr Buchanan?" Don interrupted, incredulous. He waved towards the window. "Have you not missed London? Surely your wife-to-be will learn to love the city after spending three weeks in it!"

The entire board nodded in agreement. It was becoming quickly apparent that Murdoch was not going to be able to voice his opinion that the Darrow land should be left well alone during this particular meeting, which meant he needed more time. He suppressed a sigh and smiled.

"Of course. You are right. Miss Darrow will enjoy her time here, I'm sure. As to wedding her in three weeks...well, better to leave that up to her, I think."

"Don't be ridiculous," Gregory said. "You've given the girl far more leeway than you should have ever given her. It's time you put your foot down on the matter, Mr Buchanan, and lock her down."

Keep your temper in check, Murdoch thought,

taking care to breathe deeply and evenly. He did not like the way Gregory MacKinnon spoke of Sorcha, nor the way everyone else agreed with him. He wished for her to meet them even less than he had before, though Murdoch knew he had no choice in the matter. They would find a way to meet Sorcha regardless of what he wanted, so it was better for it to be on his own terms.

"Speaking of locking Miss Darrow down," Murdoch said, hating the sentence even as he said it, "I must find her before she spends all of my money. London fashion is expensive, after all."

"See, she will fall for London before you know it, and then she will be happy that you grant her land over to us to oversee," Don exclaimed, a smug smile on his face. Clearly he thought himself far cleverer than he actually was, and would probably credit himself with the success of the entire land deal when it was complete.

Which it never will be, Murdoch swore, saying his goodbyes before exiting the meeting room and storming down the corridor. *To think they were going to strong-arm Sorcha into giving up the land. They had already given up on their expectation that Mr Buchanan would hand it over. I must be careful, and so must Sorcha.*

"I hate this place," Murdoch grumbled, for nobody to hear but himself. "I wish we could go home." But until said home was safe Murdoch knew he was stuck in London, with its detestable people, busy streets and filthy air.

That only made him hate it even more.

CHAPTER ELEVEN

Sorcha

"I never thought shopping would be so *exhausting*!" Sorcha complained to Mrs Ferguson, who had accompanied her on her excursion to buy clothes more appropriate for London.

They had visited no fewer than ten shops and had purchased items from eight of them: high-necked, long-sleeved day dresses; low-cut, gathered-sleeve evening gowns; richly-coloured silk scarves and shawls; delicate slipper-like shoes that Sorcha would never have worn back home, and bonnets, gloves and bags in an array of different finishes and sizes.

A long, woollen riding coat was the final purchase of the morning, since it was popular in the city to wear riding attire when one was not actually riding a horse. Sorcha found this especially baffling. She felt entirely insubstantial in her borrowed coat and cotton dress – which had both been Mrs Ferguson's once upon a time – now that she knew what she was supposed to be wearing, though in truth she felt far more comfortable in the servant's clothing than she perhaps ever would in the garments Murdoch Buchanan's money had bought.

But on the other hand, Sorcha thought, glancing critically at her reflection, *perhaps Murdoch will pay more attention to me if I put in some effort with my appearance.* For it was clear to Sorcha that the kelpie was keeping his distance from her, and she had no idea why. It did not seem to matter that she undressed in front of him, and told him that he looked good, and tried to sneak into his arms whilst they were in bed. Nothing seemed to sway him.

Has spending time with me away from his home caused Murdoch to realise I am not who he thought I was? Sorcha wondered, smoothing back errant strands of hair self-consciously as she continued down Oxford Street with Mrs Ferguson. *I had been sure he still felt something for me when we reunited. Was I...wrong?*

"It is a good thing your clothes will be ready by next week," Mrs Ferguson said, pulling Sorcha out of her negative thoughts. "I do not think I could carry much more than these hats and shoes!" She struggled with a pile of boxes in her arms, having staunchly refused Sorcha's multiple offers to help her with them.

Sorcha looked up at the sky; it was a beautiful day, and only a little past noon. She was not yet hungry, and she didn't feel like going back to Murdoch's house to while away the rest of the day indoors. She glanced at Mrs Ferguson. "You can return to Mr Buchanan's abode, Mrs Ferguson," she said. "I wish to explore the city for a while."

But the servant shook her head. "I cannot leave you on your own, Miss Darrow. You do not know your way around!"

74

"I have memorised Mr Buchanan's maps of London," Sorcha insisted. "And you have all those heavy boxes. I will be quite content on my own, I swear."

The woman eyed her suspiciously. Sorcha could tell what she was thinking – that a lowly country girl was sure to lose herself in the sprawling streets of Britain's largest city. But that was half of the appeal for Sorcha. She *wanted* an adventure, to see things that she had not seen before. And, after two years of bearing witness to the wonders of the Seelie Court, it was high time Sorcha gave the marvels of human ingenuity and architecture a chance.

Eventually Mrs Ferguson relented with a heavy sigh. "Do not stray far," she warned. "Stay close to Oxford Street where you can. If you ever get lost, enter a shop and ask for directions – do *not* approach anybody on the street, especially if they appear uncouth or –"

"I understand," Sorcha laughed, tightening her borrowed jacket against her chest when a bitter breeze blew past her. "I have visited Glasgow before; this is not my first time in a city."

Mrs Ferguson did not seem reassured by this, though she protested no further. With a final goodbye she turned from Sorcha to head back to Murdoch's house, leaving her alone for the first time in four days.

I do not know where the time has gone, Sorcha thought as she took a right turn and began traipsing down a pretty cobblestone street. *It feels as if it has been stolen from me.* When she passed a bakery she stared at the cakes and pastries in the window, though she did not wish to eat one. A towering bowl of sugar plums glittered in the noonday sun, distinctly reminding Sorcha of the

75

gemstones that lined the path to the Seelie Court.

A flash of light crossed the glass, and Sorcha frowned. "Definitely not the sun," she murmured, resisting the urge to touch the window out of sheer curiosity. This wasn't the first window she had caught glimmering and glinting in a way it shouldn't have been. *Perhaps the grime and smoke in the air affects the way light hits glass,* she thought, though Sorcha wasn't so sure. She had caught a similarly odd show of light in the mirror of her own home before leaving for London, after all.

"I cannot dismiss these as sleep-deprived hallucinations," she said, turning from the window with an uncomfortable, hollow pit in her stomach. Sorcha began to whistle softly in an effort to calm her nerves as she wound further away from Oxford Street without really knowing where she was going. But as she passed more shop windows and glass lanterns and mirrored surfaces she became certain that there was something wrong with what was being reflected back at her. There were odd, unexplained lights...

And eerie, fleeting shadows.

"I am imagining it," Sorcha said, louder than was strictly necessary. A passing gentleman looked at her strangely, so she scurried off the street to another, and then another and another, until Sorcha was all alone on a street with no windows at all. That should have reassured her, but it only set Sorcha's nerves further on edge. She had clearly come upon an *uncouth* area, as Mrs Ferguson would have put it, and she had no idea how to get back to where she started.

So much for memorising Murdoch's maps, Sorcha mused, heart racing with every turn she took onto new, even further abandoned streets. Fog was beginning to roll across the cobblestones, which made Sorcha think that perhaps she was close to the Thames. *If I can get to the river I can find my way back to Murdoch's house. I can do this.*

But as Sorcha walked on and on she realised she was getting ever further from anything she could hope to use as a landmark to help her find the river. She was turned entirely on her head, and with the sun at a noonday position Sorcha was finding it difficult to tell north from south.

"And now I cannot see it at all," she complained, shivering when a blanket of cloud appeared as if from nowhere to obscure most of the sky in the space of ten minutes. It only caused the fog to grow thicker across the street, until Sorcha was almost convinced it was entirely solid matter.

Sing for us, girlie.

She froze.

"Is someone there?" Sorcha asked, hating the way her voice trembled as she spoke. She hitched up the skirt of her dress a few inches from the ground, ready to flee at any given moment. But there was nobody there, and when Sorcha turned onto the next street not a soul was there, either.

Just one song, pretty lass, another voice insisted. *One song for your love.*

"L-leave me alone," Sorcha stuttered, flinching when she caught a shadow out of the corner of her eye that appeared to be moving. Her footsteps grew quicker and more insistent, though the fog absorbed the sound the soles of her shoes made against the cobblestones.

Everything was oppressively, dangerously silent.

A song, a third voice asked. *One and we shall leave you. A verse.*

Sorcha took a deep breath. She did not know what was going on, but she'd had enough experience in the faerie realm to know that what was currently happening was decidedly not the work of a human. *"L-lost is my quiet forever,"* she began, voice uneven and frightened as she sang the first song that popped into her head. She desperately searched around for an escape.

There was none.

All around her the fog and shadows began to shift, as if they were restless and excited. Sorcha knew she had to be careful, but now that she had begun singing she found that the next words in the verse left her tongue before she could stop them.

"Lost is life's happiest part;

Lost all my tender endeavours,

To touch an insensible heart."

Sorcha fled down a narrow alleyway, regretting the decision the moment she realised she could easily become boxed into it. A shadow flitted across her vision, then another and another.

"But tho' my despair is past – leave me alone!" Sorcha screamed, beyond terrified, when a hand appeared from nowhere to yank her out of the alleyway by her wrist. Freezing, bitter tears were streaming down her face, obscuring her vision. "Let me go!" she cried. "Please, let me go."

But the stranger did not release her. He was wrapped up against the cold from head to toe, though a few strands of silvered hair poked out between his woollen cap and scarf. Wordlessly he pulled on Sorcha's arm with a strength that belied the aged colour of his hair; Sorcha had no choice but to follow him.

He wove his way down street after street, waving away shadows and odd reflections in a discomfitingly spritely manner whenever they presented themselves before him. Within ten minutes Sorcha found herself back on Oxford Street, several shops away from where she had started her dangerous adventure.

"I – thank you," she mouthed, but no sound came out. Her chest ached from the force of her heart battering against her ribcage; she barely dared to breathe.

The strange old man – who was perhaps not so old at all – merely inclined his head politely and promptly disappeared down an alleyway, leaving Sorcha all alone once more. But the shadows were gone. The glimmers of light had disappeared.

The danger had passed...for now.

"Lachlan," Sorcha cried miserably before she could stop herself. "Lachlan, help me."

CHAPTER TWELVE

Murdoch

There was only one word to describe Sorcha's behaviour over the past two days: listless.

When she returned from her shopping trip and retired straight to bed Murdoch had been suspicious, especially since she spoke not a single word to either him or Mrs Ferguson when they checked up on her. Mrs Ferguson had informed him that Sorcha insisted upon exploring the city on her own, which he had bristled at, but the servant also said that Sorcha had been gone for under two hours – barely any time at all to walk around London before heading back to Murdoch's house.

Sorcha had remained quiet and morose since then, fidgeting constantly and finding herself distracted by seemingly nothing at all whilst in the middle of reading a book, or brushing her hair, or eating a meal.

She had barely touched her food at all.

And now they were sitting at the dining table in silence, and Murdoch did not know what to say. In truth

Sorcha's new-found awkwardness had been a blessing in disguise, for it made it easier for him to keep his distance.

He fiddled with a heavy, ivory card between his hands; both of them had been invited to a company luncheon at the weekend, and Murdoch was concerned that Sorcha would not fare well at the event in her current condition. He hid a heavy sigh by gulping down a large measure of red wine.

"What is it?" Sorcha asked, voice so quiet Murdoch barely heard her. She was staring at the card he was holding, a slight frown creasing her brow. "You have been looking at that all evening."

Murdoch handed it over to her. "Grey and MacKinnon have invited us to join the company for a luncheon on Saturday. I was not sure if you would like to go."

"Of course I'm going!" Sorcha insisted, more lively than she had been in two days. "I *have* to go, otherwise I will not be able to get the measure of these men who wish to take our home away."

"You must be careful around them, Sorcha," Murdoch replied, taking another sip of wine as he did so. "They will not treat you the same way the people of Darach do."

She rolled her eyes. "Of course I know that. My mother would kill me if I wasn't on my best behaviour down here."

"I wasn't aware you could *be* on your best behaviour."

The hint of a smile curled Sorcha's lips, and Murdoch began to relax. Whatever had been burdening her seemed finally to be passing, for which he was grateful. "You will be able to wear your new clothes," he said, eager to keep up their new-found line of pleasant conversation. "And Mrs Ferguson can help with your hair, so you do not need to worry over it."

"Was that a not-so-subtle attempt at telling me my hair is a mess?" Sorcha asked, running her fingers through her admittedly disastrously tangled locks until she hit a snag and winced.

He laughed. "You and I both know I do not care how you present yourself; it is merely others that do."

"You don't?"

"Of course not," Murdoch said, confused by the question. *When have I ever given Sorcha reason to think that I am superficial? And she is beautiful, anyway, particularly when her hair is wild around her face.* He thought of the faerie revel, when he had slain Lachlan's step family. Sorcha's hair had been braided through with bluebells, so delicate that they whispered to the floor whenever Murdoch had touched her.

He pushed the memory away.

There was a strange look on Sorcha's face, as if she was unsure if Murdoch was lying to her or not about her appearance being unimportant to him. But then she shook her head, picked up her fork and began to eat, much to Murdoch's immense relief.

When they were finished eating the two of them retired to the drawing room, sitting in front of a merrily blazing hearth to read and relax. Sorcha was scanning through reams of music she had found by the piano Mr Buchanan's father used to play, though the instrument was in desperate need of tuning from two years of disuse.

She hummed softly as her fingers trailed across notes and bars and verses, occasionally vocalising entire phrases when she came upon ones she particularly liked.

"I have missed your singing," Murdoch said after a while, closing the heavy book on English law that he was reading with a thump. Sorcha looked up at him from where she lay sprawled across the carpet, dark hair flickering and glowing like burnished copper wire in the light of the flames. Her cheeks were flushed, and they only grew redder in response to Murdoch's comment.

"I did not dare sing by the loch, after what happened," she admitted, turning her mismatched eyes to the fire. "I only sang for Lachlan – and Galileo, of course. I hope he is all right on the MacPherson farm."

A surge of jealousy wracked through Murdoch's body. He did not want to know that Sorcha continued to sing for the Seelie king, but in his heart he'd always known she would. It was how Lachlan had met her, after all, something which Murdoch had gleaned from Sorcha's thoughts the first time he'd spoken to her in the water of Loch Lomond.

She had been singing to me a long time before he met her, Murdoch thought glumly. *Yet it is the faerie who has become indispensable in Sorcha's life.*

He scratched his chin, where a fine layer of stubble was beginning to grow. Murdoch wanted to shave, but he didn't have the energy to. There was an unbearable, itching dryness creeping through his veins and threatening to desiccate his very being. He knew he needed to swim; to be part of a body of water and feel himself again.

Right now, in the middle of winter and posing as Murdoch Buchanan, that was impossible.

"What has been on your mind the last couple of days, Sorcha?" he asked before he could stop himself. Her eyes had grown glassy as they stared into the fire. She almost looked transfixed, but when she realised Murdoch had asked her a question she blinked life back into her eyes.

"I...may have been followed when I was walking about alone," she said, very slowly. She did not meet Murdoch's gaze, as if she were afraid of his reaction.

His hand curled into a taut fist in his lap before he could stop himself. "Followed?" he echoed back. "Did you see who it was?"

Sorcha shook her head. "No, I don't know who it was, but I was lost and –"

"You cannot act so reckless down here!" Murdoch exclaimed, dropping from his chair to kneel in front of her. Sorcha pushed herself up into a sitting position, running a hand through her hair to push it out of her face as she did so.

She bit her lip. "I was all right in the end," she said, a little uncertainly. "An old man helped me back to Oxford Street and –"

Murdoch grabbed onto her arms before he could stop himself. He was angry at Sorcha, and scared for her. He shook her slightly. "You must be more careful, Sorcha!" he insisted. "London is a dangerous city. You could get hurt!"

"Do you think I don't know that?" she demanded, growing angry herself. "I am not a child, Murdoch. I know what I did was foolish. Why do you think I hadn't told you about it yet?"

A moment of silence passed. Two. Three.

84

Murdoch let out a long, low breath through gritted teeth. His shoulders slumped. "I apologise," he said. "Really, I am sorry. I do not mean to be so short with you."

"It is my own fault," Sorcha admitted, holding Murdoch's gaze as she shifted closer to him. "London is doing strange things to me. I feel so out of sorts."

He barked out a laugh. "You have just described precisely how I feel, too."

Sorcha glanced downward at Murdoch's hands, still gripping her forearms. Her dress had slipped from one shoulder, the material just barely covering her breasts as she shifted her sitting position. A heat that had entirely nothing to do with his proximity to the fire burned through Murdoch, and his grip tightened.

I must let her go, he thought, though his eyes were trained on Sorcha's lower lip as she ran the tip of her tongue across it. She leaned a little closer towards him.

"Murdoch," she began, voice low and lilting and full of something Murdoch thought might be agonisingly close to desire, "what are we –"

He pushed her away. "I should prepare some documents for my meeting tomorrow," he muttered, standing up without looking at Sorcha. But out of the corner of his eye Murdoch saw a look of humiliation creep across her face, which hadn't been his intention at all. *I did not mean to hurt her,* he worried, *but I am not myself right now.* "Sorcha –" Murdoch said, but he cut her off with a wave of her hand.

"I am tired," she bit out, dragging herself to her feet and fleeing the drawing room without waiting for a response. Murdoch stood frozen to the spot for a moment, torn by indecision, before finally bounding out after her.

"Sorcha," he said again, "I did not mean to offend you. It's just – Sorcha?"

When Murdoch reached his bedroom he found Sorcha half-draped across the bed, thoroughly unconscious. His eye twitched, and his hand curled into a fist once more. Frustrated, he kicked at a chest of drawers and cursed loudly, before very carefully placing Sorcha on the bed properly and wrapping her beneath the covers. The hint of a smile was on her lips; gone was all her anger at Murdoch.

He was beyond jealous, for there was only one creature who could have done this to Sorcha, and he could do nothing to rouse her.

Murdoch had no choice but to wait for Lachlan to allow Sorcha to wake from her enchanted sleep.

CHAPTER THIRTEEN

Lachlan

"Lachlan! I knew it had to be you. I have not fallen asleep so abruptly in a long time."

The flood of relief that washed over Lachlan upon seeing Sorcha was overwhelming. And she was *happy* to see him. Delighted and relieved, going by the way she bounded into his arms and melted against his chest.

The kelpie has not turned her on me yet, he thought, viciously pleased. *And he never will.*

He extended their embrace for longer than was strictly necessary, simply because he did not want to let go. Sorcha made no indication she wanted to let go, either, but eventually the pair of them acknowledged that clinging to each other was hardly the easiest way to talk to one another. So Lachlan released her, but not before he kissed her forehead softly.

"I hope I did not catch you at a bad time," Lachlan said, smiling at the sheer vision that was the human in front of him. Sorcha's hair was in such familiar disarray it made his heart ache. "It is hard to keep track of the hour when it is dark for so much of the day."

For a moment Lachlan almost thought that Sorcha blushed, but then she scowled and fell backwards into the soft, vague darkness of her dream. "Not a bad time," she told him. "Ideal timing, in fact."

Lachlan collapsed beside her, an intrigued eyebrow raised. "How so? Have you grown tired of your horse husband yet?"

Sorcha snorted at the comment, which in turn caused Lachlan to laugh. Already he could feel his very soul relaxing by her proximity. *Indulging in easy, non-judgemental conversation that has absolutely nothing to do with ruling a kingdom certainly helps lift my mood, too.*

"I think he may be tired of me, in all honesty," Sorcha murmured in answer to his question.

"I do not believe that for a moment."

"Well he's putting on an excellent show of it, then," she huffed, blowing stray strands of hair out of her face in the process. She glanced at Lachlan, her blue and green eyes pale mirrors against the darkness of her dream. "It is as if Murdoch can barely stand to have me near."

Oh.

Lachlan worked out what that meant immediately. He didn't know how to feel about it – that the kelpie was keeping Sorcha at arm's length because he didn't want to push his feelings onto her. *I didn't realise he had a single ounce of maturity beneath all his possessiveness. I suppose you don't live to be five hundred without learning how to hold your feelings in check. He is more of a foe for Sorcha's heart than I gave him credit for.*

"Lachlan?"

He smiled at her reassuringly, reaching out to stroke Sorcha's hand with his own. "I am here, do not worry."

Her eyes narrowed. "But *how* are you here? I am hundreds of miles away! Do not tell me you've travelled all the way down and –"

"Oh, for the love of the forest, no," he chuckled. "Ailith would kill me if she realised I'd gone gallivanting down to London before the solstice revel."

"So how...?"

"My powers have grown since I became king," Lachlan explained. He flexed and unflexed a golden hand above his head, allowing his very being to glow from within for Sorcha's benefit. She reached up to touch his palm; sparks flew from where her fingertips grazed his skin.

She gasped at the marvel of it all. "Does that mean you put me to sleep and invaded my dreams all the way from the Seelie Court?" she asked, eyes shining with interest.

Lachlan flashed her a grin. "I did not expect it to work – I have been trying for several days with no success – though I am sincerely glad that it did. So tell me, Clara: how goes things down in London? Have you and the horse made much progress getting Grey and MacKinnon to back down?"

"Not exactly," she admitted. "Murdoch is doing his best to convince them to leave the land alone – I swear he is – but they will not budge. They look at Loch Lomond and the Darrow land and see a goldmine."

Lachlan did not like the sound of that. "These men could be dangerous," he said. "Please tell me you are being careful – that the kelpie is keeping you out of harm's reach." *It is the very least the monster could do, after all.*

"In truth I have not met them yet, though the company is hosting a luncheon this weekend that I am expected to attend."

"You are not nervous, are you?" Lachlan laughed incredulously at the slight frown creasing Sorcha's brow. He rolled onto his front and propped himself up on his elbows, then flicked his thumb and forefinger against her frown until Sorcha, too, was laughing. "Come on, Clara," he continued. "You live in the company of faeries and kelpies. You have witnessed beheadings and drownings and curses and you are nervous of mere *humans?*"

"Strangers," Sorcha muttered, averting her eyes. "They are strangers. I do not do well with strangers, especially ones from London meaning to convince me into handing over everything I am trying to protect."

"I was a stranger, once. So was your kelpie."

Sorcha shifted onto her side to face Lachlan. "You are strange, but you were never a stranger. The forest and loch are both as familiar to me as my parents are." But beneath the lovely smile she had painted on her face Lachlan could tell that Sorcha's entire body was tense, as if ready to bolt at any given second.

He edged closer to her. "But there are other strangers, aren't they? Do not lie to me; I can see it on your face. What is wrong, Sorcha?"

Sorcha's eyes widened at Lachlan's use of her real name, for he only used it when he was truly serious. She bit her lip, which was trembling slightly. "There is something...different about London," she eventually said. "I do not know how to explain it. Reflections and shadows all feel wrong, somehow. Like they're keeping something from me and taunting me at the same time."

Lachlan pinned Sorcha beneath him before he truly knew what he was doing, catching her wrists in his hands and squeezing them tightly. "Do not go near them!" he barked, feeling a panic rise in his throat that he had not felt since he was a fox. "The moment something feels wrong, *run*. Do not walk anywhere in London without the kelpie."

"You - Lachlan - what is wrong? What exactly are the shadows?" Sorcha's chest was heaving in fright; clearly she had not expected such a visceral reaction from him.

"It could well be the Unseelie," Lachlan said. His grip on her wrists tightened even further. "Sorcha, I am being serious here. *Do not take this lightly.* If you think something is in your head then it isn't. It never is with them. They are the worst kinds of faeries to become involved with - you won't just lose your time or your memories or your tears to them. Do not give them anything, for you will lose everything and more."

Slowly, very slowly, Sorcha nodded. "I will be careful, I swear it," she told him. "I will not run off on my own."

Relieved that Sorcha had truly understood the gravity of his warning, Lachlan let go of her wrists and collapsed on top of her. He nuzzled his face against her neck. "You did not break my step family's curse only for me to lose you to the damn Unseelie," he muttered. "I will not have it. You are not theirs to take."

Sorcha ran a hand over the back of Lachlan's hair. The gesture was soothing enough that he found himself moulding his body to Sorcha's, sliding a leg between hers to lessen the pressure of his weight on her chest. They lay like that, content not to move, and listened to each other do naught but breathe for a long, long time.

"I am nobody's to take," Sorcha eventually whispered. "I only belong to me."

Lachlan grazed his lips across Sorcha's jawline. "That is the biggest problem of all."

"You do not truly mean that."

"I do. I cannot lie, as well you know."

Sorcha did not reply to Lachlan's easy admission of possessiveness. *Perhaps the kelpie is not so dissimilar to me,* he reasoned. *I thought I could accept Sorcha being mortal and living a human life, but I can't. It isn't enough. It never will be.*

For Sorcha's continued trust and affection of him, it had to be.

"Will you stay with me tonight?" she asked, when Lachlan finally rolled off her to rest her head against his chest.

He placed a gentle kiss upon her brow. "I would stay with you forever, if you would only let me."

CHAPTER FOURTEEN

Murdoch

Murdoch watched as Sorcha struggled to fasten the buttons running up the back of her bodice by herself. He wanted to help, but was terrified of touching her.

The image of her sleeping, enchanted face was burned into his retinas. Whenever Murdoch thought about Lachlan spending the night with Sorcha inside her dreams he found he could barely control his temper. Watching Sorcha get dressed did not help matters at all.

They were late for Grey and MacKinnon's luncheon, but Murdoch didn't have it in him to be concerned. There was no way he was going to be able to talk to them about giving up the Darrow land whilst they were feasting and drinking and socialising, anyway; all Murdoch could do was introduce them to Sorcha and hope that they were as enamoured with her as he was.

Not that I want that, either, he grumbled, a shiver running down his spine at the thought of any of the board members eyeing up Sorcha. *But if she charms*

them then they may be inclined to give up on their
Loch Lomond plans.

He laughed humourlessly. Something like that was never going to happen.

Sorcha cast a curious glance his way, which was the closest Murdoch had gotten to holding eye contact with her for three days. "What is so funny?" she asked.

"Nothing. Do you need some help?"

She shook her head, the apples of her cheeks turning pink as she twisted her arms behind her back to finish fastening the buttons. Sorcha's periwinkle dress was cut low across her breastbone and cinched in high up on her waist, with delicate, floral embroidery decorating the bodice and matching, elbow-length gloves to complete the look. Her hair was twisted elegantly at the nape of her neck, with a few artfully curled tendrils left hanging to frame her face. A darker blue, silken shawl was hanging over the mirror, obscuring her reflection from view.

"You look beautiful," Murdoch said when Sorcha turned to face him. It was painfully true; her delicate, sloping shoulders and pale skin perfectly balanced the wintry-coloured ensemble.

Sorcha ignored the compliment, grabbing the shawl before moving past Murdoch towards the door. "Come on," she mumbled, "we are late enough as it is."

He grabbed Sorcha's wrist before he could stop himself. She glared at him until Murdoch let her go. "We cannot act like this in front of my - in front of Mr Buchanan's colleagues," he insisted, though that was not what Murdoch wanted to say at all. *How can it be so difficult to tell her that I'm sorry? That I'm deathly jealous of Lachlan stealing into her dreams, and that the last thing I wanted to do was push her away into his arms?*

But Murdoch did not say these things.

Sorcha stared at him with hard, searching eyes for a moment or two, then bowed her head and sighed. "I know," she said. "I know. Our home depends on it."

When she offered him a small smile Murdoch eagerly returned it. But despite their mutual agreement that they could not act so cold to each other, neither of them spoke a word during the carriage ride over to Howard Grey's ostentatiously large townhouse in the middle of Mayfair. Every time Murdoch came close to asking Sorcha about Lachlan he fidgeted with his sleeve, instead, or fiddled with the silver pocket-watch Mr Buchanan's father had once gifted his son.

Sorcha was equally restless, looking out the window of the carriage every two or three minutes only to dart her eyes away from the glass as if she had seen something monstrous or disturbing outside. Once or twice she opened her mouth to speak but, just as with Murdoch, she thought better of it before any words were formed.

It was with great relief that their carriage rolled up to Mr Grey's house having made good time; they were but ten minutes late. Murdoch exited the carriage first, crunching across the gravelled driveway to help Sorcha down from her side of it. She took hold of his hand without so much as a flinch, an angelic smile plastered to her face.

"Thank you, Mr Buchanan," she said without an ounce of animosity. She linked her arm with Murdoch's, knocking the top of her head affectionately against his shoulder before allowing him to lead her through a set of tall, heavy brass doors.

A servant led them up a flight of stairs heavily decorated with grand, ostentatious portraits of the men of the house of Grey. Sorcha stared at each of them with a glint of mischief in her eyes.

Murdoch squeezed her hand softly and whispered into her ear, "Just what are you thinking, Miss Darrow?"

"That you are far more handsome than any of these portraits, Mr Buchanan."

He snickered softly at the comment. "I wouldn't say that to Howard Grey's face. You might break his poor heart!"

"Oh, the horror! I would never dare do such a thing," Sorcha murmured back, holding a hand over her mouth to stifle a wicked laugh as the two of them were brought into a very large, high-ceilinged, extravagantly decorated dining room. But there was no table sitting in the centre of the room; instead, trestle tables covered in pristine, white cloths were set against the walls and were laden with all manner of bite-size morsels, with several servants on-hand to pile plates high with food and pour drinks.

There were around thirty people filtering around the room, with two more appearing from a door at the opposite end that led to another part of the house. At Murdoch's side Sorcha gulped almost imperceptibly and closed her eyes for a moment, steeling herself for the onslaught of strangers.

Murdoch felt a stab of sympathy for his fake wife-to-be; for all Sorcha's insistence that she would be fine, it was clear that she truly did not like strangers. *How I must have scared her when first we met simply by being a man rather than a creature from the deep,* he thought, feeling somewhat guilty about having originally enjoyed her fear. Murdoch resolved himself to put Sorcha at ease in any way he could.

"Would you like a drink, Miss Da-"

"Murdoch, you're late!" Howard called over the noise of the room, cutting through the crowd with the speed of a man half his age. Going by his ruddy cheeks Murdoch could only assume the man was already halfway drunk.

"My deepest apologies," he said, bowing his head.

"It is my fault," Sorcha chimed in, smiling a brilliant smile for the older man before curtsying. She turned her smile on Murdoch before saying, "It is all my fault that we are late. I simply couldn't decide what to wear!"

Howard beamed at her, reaching for Sorcha's hand with both of his own. "You can only be Miss Darrow, the charming lass who stole our Mister Buchanan away from us!" he exclaimed. "It is a pleasure to finally meet you."

"All things considered, the pleasure is mine, Mister...?"

"Howard Grey," Murdoch cut in, remembering his own manners. "Howard, this is indeed Sorcha Darrow. Miss Darrow, this is the co-founder of Grey and MacKinnon, Howard Grey."

"I should have known someone of such distinction was the man who owned this house," Sorcha told Howard, before thanking a servant who proffered her a glass of champagne. She looked at the contents of the glass curiously – Murdoch could only assume she had never been given the opportunity to drink such a beverage before.

Neither have I, technically, he thought, taking a glass for himself and cautiously taking a sip. The sweet alcohol fizzed and bubbled on his tongue, a bizarre sensation Murdoch was unsure whether he enjoyed or not.

Howard laughed heartily at Sorcha's remark, approval plain as day on his face. "I like you, Miss Darrow, though if you continue to ply me with such compliments then I may be inclined to steal you away for myself!"

And so it was that Murdoch watched as Sorcha charmed her way around each and every one of the board members of Grey and MacKinnon, discussing atlases with James Campbell and ships with William Wright, then moving on to discuss the works of Robert Burns with an attentive Donald MacKinnon. Murdoch resisted the urge to step in and whisk Sorcha away, for the entire purpose of bringing her to the luncheon was for her to meet everyone.

But still, I do not like it.

"Jealousy is unseemly, Mr Buchanan." Murdoch flinched; Don's father had sidled up beside him, a sly smile on his face. He inclined his head towards Sorcha. "I can certainly see why you were loathe to return to London, though I must profess I believed that no woman could tie *you* down. And a lowly country girl, no less! I am truly surprised. Though she is certainly holding her own this afternoon. Her mother must have worked hard to give her a respectable upbringing."

Murdoch struggled to maintain a neutral demeanour. "The Darrows are fine people," he said. "They have been nothing but welcoming to me. And Miss Darrow –"

"Has clearly put you firmly under her spell," Gregory laughed, though his eyes were sharp and serious. "Just remember, Mr Buchanan, that you are marrying the girl for a reason. Do not allow yourself to be swept away."

The man walked away once he had voiced his opinion, leaving Murdoch to watch Sorcha with a heavy cloud hanging above him. *The more time I spend as Mr Buchanan the more I despise him,* he thought glumly, tilting the rest of his champagne down his throat. *London turned him into a womanising, parasitic businessman. I am glad I ate him.*

But it only served to further conflict Murdoch over the matter of his feelings for Sorcha. He could not stand the person he was pretending to be; to touch her using the skin he was borrowing was unthinkable. Murdoch could scarcely believe he had once thought the vessel a suitable one for him to possess.

"I would never have met her the way I did without him," Murdoch whispered, so quietly even he struggled to hear the words. He wondered if Sorcha would still accept him if he took on another face; another voice; another body. *Or is her attraction to me predicated on me looking like this?*

Murdoch did not want to consider that at all, but by the time he worked that out it was too late – it was all he could think about. When he caught his moody reflection in his empty champagne glass he scowled.

"I hate you."

CHAPTER FIFTEEN

Sorcha

Sorcha hadn't experienced such deafening silence since she'd returned from her stint as a runaway and had to bear the brunt of her parents' abject disappointment in her. Murdoch wasn't the only one responsible for it, of course; Sorcha was equally to blame for the arctic atmosphere between the two of them.

After they'd successfully acted as a happy couple at Howard Grey's luncheon Sorcha had thought that, perhaps, she and Murdoch would be able to bridge the gap that had formed between them. Instead it had only grown wider.

Why did he push me away? Sorcha thought sullenly, aimlessly pushing around the chicken on her plate with no intention whatsoever of eating it. She was alone; Murdoch had locked himself in his office, working through another book of English law to try and find some decree or case that could help him force his work colleagues to back off from procuring the Darrow land. Murdoch was staying quiet on his progress, which only caused Sorcha to believe that he was trying to protect her from something.

"Or simply wishes to keep me out of it," she grumbled, stabbing a potato so violently that it broke into pieces. *It is as if he wants nothing to do with me. Just what is going on?* Sorcha was sure she hadn't imagined the way Murdoch looked at her when they sat by the fire and she confessed to having been followed. And when they'd pretended to be happily engaged at the work luncheon she'd thought his affection for her was genuine.

Now Sorcha was considering that it truly was all an act. Or that, at least, whatever feelings the kelpie once held for her were long gone.

She sighed heavily. It certainly didn't help that Murdoch was tetchy and irritable most of the time, and that aside from heading out for work meetings he did not get out of the house at all. Sorcha herself was sticking to Lachlan's advice not to go anywhere without Murdoch in tow and had subsequently not left the house for days, either, which didn't serve to improve her mood.

But Murdoch was much worse.

There must be something seriously wrong, Sorcha thought, picking up her mostly uneaten dinner and carrying it through to the kitchen. Mrs Ferguson was nowhere to be found, which suggested she was eating her own dinner elsewhere, so Sorcha tended to her dishes and washed whatever was left by the basin, too. A large tub of water was hanging over a fire; Sorcha stood and stared at it boiling for a few minutes simply because she had nothing else to do.

And then it hit her.

"Water!" Sorcha cried, feeling stupid for not having realised it earlier. Murdoch was a kelpie, and he had said himself it had been a long, long time since he'd ventured away from his home. The last time he'd lived as Murdoch Buchanan he had been by the loch at all times, and shifted back and forth into his original form.

London had so far been cold, grey and, above all, bone dry. Sorcha's hair had suffered from the harsh conditions, which meant she could only imagine how Murdoch's entire being was faring.

"Oh, my, Miss Darrow, let me wash those!" Mrs Ferguson exclaimed, horrified to enter the kitchen and discover that she had largely finished the dishes. "You should be spending time with Mr Buchanan, not acting as his servant."

"Mrs Ferguson," Sorcha said, ignoring the woman's protests. "Would you be able to fill the tub in the main bathroom? The really large one?"

"It will take at least two hours for it to heat up properly," Mrs Ferguson said, "would it not be better to use the smaller tub in Mr Buchanan's private bathroom?"

"It doesn't need to be very hot," Sorcha countered. She pointed at the water boiling over the fire. "And if you put some of that in the bath then it will take even less time to do so. You can retire for the evening when it is run."

The servant nodded. "As you wish, Miss Darrow. I will prepare the bath immediately."

Sorcha paced the drawing room impatiently as Mrs Ferguson got to work, half-heartedly reading an encyclopaedia entry on Egyptian hieroglyphs before putting the tome down to stare through the darkened window at the empty street below. It felt like hours passed before Mrs Ferguson knocked on the door to inform Sorcha that the bath was ready. She thanked the woman, sent her to her own quarters, then took a deep breath.

Here goes nothing, she thought, hesitating with her fist against the door of Murdoch's study. *If he turns me away then there is nothing I can do...except use the bath myself.*

She knocked upon the door. No response. She knocked again.

"Murdoch?" she called through the wood. "Murdoch, do you –"

"What is it, Sorcha?" Murdoch asked, swinging open the door as he spoke. Sorcha took a step back from him in surprise. She swept her gaze over his dishevelled, exhausted appearance.

"Your hair is more of a mess than mine usually is," she said, smiling despite the fact neither of them had spoken in days.

Murdoch ran a hand over his face. "I don't see much point in tidying it when I do not intend to leave the house nor entertain guests tonight," he said. "Was there something you needed, Sorcha?"

She shifted on the spot. *How on earth do I tell a kelpie I think he's dehydrated?* Eventually she reached out, grabbed Murdoch's wrist and pulled on it. "Just follow me," she said, knowing that if Murdoch did not want to move then no amount of hauling and dragging would enable Sorcha to shift his towering frame. But Murdoch, blessedly, obliged, wordlessly following

Sorcha until she stopped inside the main bathroom.

The metal tub inside was so large Sorcha reckoned she could have fit Galileo inside of it. It was filled two-thirds of the way with lightly steaming, cloudy water; clearly Mrs Ferguson had poured in some mineral salts. She pointed towards it for lack of anything else to do.

"Get in," she ordered, without looking at Murdoch.

He didn't respond for a moment, then let out a long, low laugh that filled Sorcha's heart with joy. She glanced at him; Murdoch was scratching the dark shadow of stubble that covered his chin, a small smile on his face. He shook his head in disbelief. "How did you know?" he asked.

"You've been...temperamental," Sorcha replied. "Can I assume from the look on your face that this was the right thing to do?"

"I think it may well be."

They stood there in awkward silence, both staring at the bathtub for a while until eventually Murdoch turned to Sorcha and asked, "Are you going to leave so I can get in?"

"Oh!" she cried, feeling her cheeks begin to heat up out of sheer embarrassment. "Yes, of course! Enjoy your soak!" Sorcha knew she was speaking far too quickly and far too loudly, but clearly Murdoch found the entire situation rather amusing. His dark eyes had a shine to them that Sorcha had not seen in days.

Sorcha pulled the door mostly closed behind her, fleeing down the corridor towards Murdoch's bedroom feeling entirely like an idiot. *What was I expecting to happen?* she thought, feeling disappointed nonetheless. *That he would ask me to join him? That he would take me in his arms and...I don't know.*

Once Sorcha reached the bedroom she stripped out of her day clothes and let her hair down. She collapsed onto a chair in front of Murdoch's full-length mirror and ran a soft brush through it, watching her reflection as she worked through every tangled section until it shone like burnished copper. Sorcha had avoided mirrors for days, but looking at herself now she saw that her cheeks were a little gaunt.

I should have eaten dinner, she mused, leaning over to grab the shirt she'd been wearing to bed from where she'd abandoned it on the floor that morning and tossing it on. Murdoch had encouraged her to wear the floor-length night dress that she'd bought with Mrs Ferguson the week before, but Sorcha had insisted on continuing to use his shirt regardless. She felt far more comfortable in the thigh-length fabric.

It reminded her of curling up in a tent on the shores of Loch Lomond, dreaming of foxes and kelpies and curses.

I wish I could speak to Lachlan again, Sorcha thought longingly. *I should have told him about how I sang a song for those voices.* But Sorcha did not know if her incomplete song had technically counted as having given those that had followed her what they wanted. *'Do not give them anything, for you will lose everything.' That was what Lachlan said. So did I give them anything? Is that why I can still see –*

Sorcha stopped mid-thought. In the mirror all of the long shadows in the bedroom seemed to be stretching and shifting, but when Sorcha turned to look behind her all was still and solid. Slowly, very slowly, she stood up and backed away until she could no longer see the mirror's surface. But when she passed a shiny metal decanter by the bed an impossibly fast shadow crossed its surface, followed by a flash of light.

And laughter.

In her haste to leave the bedroom Sorcha tripped over her own feet, narrowly avoiding falling flat on her face by clinging to the door. Taking a moment to catch her breath, Sorcha barely made it past the hallway mirror before she saw the shadows had followed her. They ebbed and flowed like water, with glimmering edges of silver and blue and, occasionally, white-hot gold.

"What do you *want?*" she asked some point past her pale reflection, stepping right up to the ornately-framed mirror until she was close enough that her breath fogged up the glass. She raised her trembling hands and splayed her fingertips a mere inch from the surface. *Do not touch the glass,* Sorcha thought, somehow certain that if she did then no good would come of it.

But she did not step away, and the shadows crept closer.

A song, a song, a voice called, the sound echoing all around her.

Just one song, cried another.

The rush of blood in Sorcha's ears was deafening – almost loud enough to drown out the voices, but not quite. She opened her mouth, then closed it, chewing on her lip in her desperate attempt to keep herself from singing.

Sorcha shook her head at her reflection, stumbling away from the mirror on unbalanced feet that desperately wanted her to move forwards, not back. She did not stop moving, knowing that she had to find a way to block out the voices before it was too late.

It was in this precise manner that Sorcha crashed through the bathroom door, slipped on the ceramic tiles and fell straight into the lap of a wide-eyed kelpie in the shape of Murdoch Buchanan.

CHAPTER SIXTEEN

Lachlan

Lachlan was growing worrisomely accustomed to being awake during daylight, though as the winter solstice was fast approaching there were very few such hours to actually be concerned about.

"That colour suits you, Lachlan," Ailith said from her position curled up by the fire, strumming her fingers across a handheld harp and filling the room with the delicate notes of a nameless melody.

Lachlan fussed with the large jade stone attached to his cravat until it was nestled in the hollow of his throat. He had spent the last few hours trying to decide what to wear to the winter solstice revel and, though he had gone through most every colour he could think of, Lachlan kept returning to greens and turquoises and seafoams.

Sorcha's colours.

He was wearing a pair of scandalously tight, jewel-green trousers attached over his frothy white shirt with similarly-coloured braces, which were embroidered with a delicate pattern of golden oak leaves. A pine-needle-coloured tailcoat so dark it was almost black was thrown over the back of a chair, and several pairs of boots and shoes were scattered across the floor.

Lachlan scowled. "It is no use," he complained, collapsing onto his bed in an incredibly exaggerated manner. He blew an errant strand of long, bronze-coloured hair out of his face. "It does not matter what I wear; there will be nobody at the revel I wish to impress."

With a chuckle Ailith stopped playing her harp and unfolded herself from the floor, gliding over to bend down and kiss Lachlan softly upon his lips. He reciprocated for a moment, and then another, but just when he thought Ailith might take things further she straightened up and sat beside him.

"You are thinking of Miss Sorcha," she said, a frustratingly knowing edge to her voice. "It is a good thing I have to stay here to watch the Court whilst you attend the revel, otherwise I might be deeply upset that you do not wish to impress me."

Lachlan rolled his eyes at the jibe. "Go attend to Eirian in my stead, then," he said, half-serious.

But Ailith merely shook her head and nudged Lachlan's shoulder. "What would it look like, for the King of the Seelie Court to deign not to show up to the winter solstice celebrations? You must go, Lachlan, and you know it."

"It would be a whole lot more bearable if Clara were with me," he mumbled, stretching his hands up above his head, interlacing his fingers and pushing against them until his knuckles cracked.

Ailith winced at the noise but did not comment on it. Wordlessly she pulled a sapphire-encrusted comb from her sleeve and began running it through Lachlan's hair, fanning it out on the bed like a golden halo. She stroked it gently. "Your hair is getting very long again."

"And?"

"And perhaps it is time for a change," she suggested. "Perhaps it is time for you to have the courage to actually do the things you need to do."

Lachlan swung up into a sitting position. He narrowed his eyes at her. "What is that supposed to imply?"

"Oh, Lachlan, just *ask Miss Sorcha to the revel.*"

"Just...how?"

"I know you managed to sneak into her dreams a sennight ago," Ailith said, tone disarmingly casual as she ran her comb through her hair.

Lachlan leaned forward and propped his chin up on his hands. "How did you know about that?" he mumbled, thoroughly discomfited that he'd been caught out.

But Ailith merely laughed. "It was as if a weight had been lifted from your shoulders the next day. You would have walked on air if it were possible. So put her to sleep once more and ask her to the revel."

"I cannot do that?"

"And why not?"

"Because I have tried to ease Clara into sleep more than once since then, and it has not worked."

Ailith considered this for a moment. "If you managed it once, you should be able to do it again," she said, choosing her words carefully. "Which implies that something else is blocking you from reaching her."

"I think it may be Clara herself," Lachlan admitted. "It does not seem like she is sleeping well, for whenever it feels as if I may have finally hooked her into unconsciousness she shakes it off."

"That's impressive, for a mortal."

"It is only because she is so far away," he said, throwing his head back to stare blindly up at the ceiling of his four poster bed. Gilded, gossamer fabric shone in the firelight as if it was made of liquid. "If she were close by I could put her to sleep no matter her mental state."

When Ailith squeezed his arm Lachlan did not shrug her off. "Why don't you head to London first, then, and invite Miss Sorcha to the revel face-to-face? I'm sure she would love a surprise like that. It would only add an extra day to your journey."

"I – are you serious, Ailith?"

"Very."

"I am the Seelie king," Lachlan said, gesturing at himself as he spoke. "I cannot simply gallivant off to London on a whim just to ask a mortal to –"

"It is precisely *because* you are the Seelie king that you can do whatever you want, you fool," Ailith scolded. "You have been a responsible ruler these past two years; nobody would criticise you for acting selfishly this one time. On the contrary, perhaps it would be better for you to indulge in more of your old pastimes to connect with the lower fae."

Ailith grinned a grin full of perfect, gleaming teeth at the suggestion that Lachlan was not acting nearly hedonistic enough to be a faerie king. But she was right,

Lachlan knew. After the debacle with the kelpie – after nearly losing his very being to the body of a fox at the hands of Fergus and his father – Lachlan had become an agonisingly careful creature.

It was time for that to change.

"You are right, of course," he said, a smile curling his lips to match Ailith's. "You are always right."

"That is what I am here for."

Lachlan ran a hand through her pale, perfect hair and brought Ailith's lips to his own. He just barely planted a kiss upon them. "I will bring Sorcha back with me to live in the Seelie Court, just wait and see," he murmured, his voice shaking from barely-contained excitement.

"Does that mean you're wearing the jade outfit to the revel, then?"

"Absolutely."

Ailith's nose wrinkled in amusement. "Oh, thank the forest you've decided. Now we can finally retire to bed."

For the first time in a long time Lachlan slept a sound, uninterrupted sleep, the promise of whisking Sorcha into his arms once more dancing through his dreams in a tantalising, never-ending loop.

CHAPTER SEVENTEEN

Murdoch

"Sorcha, just what are you – Sorcha?"

Murdoch didn't know what to do. One moment he was relaxing in the bath, allowing himself to quite literally dissolve in the water as his mood lifted drastically, and the next...

Sorcha had come crashing through the door and fallen straight into the tub. Going by the look on her face it hadn't been deliberate; she was pale and surprised. *And frightened,* Murdoch realised, going by how much her pupils had contracted. But the very first moment she'd fallen into the bath Sorcha had been wearing a decidedly different look on her face.

She'd almost appeared charmed.

"Sorcha?" Murdoch ventured again. When he tried to help steady her Sorcha merely collapsed with her back against his chest, shaking slightly as she looked up at him through her eyelashes.

"I'm – I saw things," she whispered. "Heard things."

Murdoch held a hand to her forehead; she was deathly cold, so he wrapped his arms around her to pull her even closer to him.

"What kind of things?" he asked. "Where did you see them?"

Sorcha didn't respond at first. She dropped her head back down to stare at the steaming, frothy bathwater swirling all around them. "...the mirrors," she finally admitted. "In the mirrors, and in the water jug, and in the windows, and in every shadowy corner I see them."

It was Murdoch's turn to feel his very core turn to ice. "The Unseelie," he said through gritted teeth. "You are seeing the Unseelie, Sorcha."

"I...thought it might be them," she said. She fidgeted with the collar of her sodden bed-shirt; Murdoch imagined it wasn't particularly comfortable to wear in a bath. Sorcha glanced back up at him. "Lachlan warned me about them when I told him about being followed through the streets."

Murdoch stiffened. He tightened his grip around Sorcha's waist. "You never mentioned anything supernatural about your being followed to me," he bit out tersely. "Why did you tell Lachlan, when he is hundreds of miles away?"

"I do not know."

She trusts him more than me, Murdoch realised. *Down here, in an unfamiliar place dealing with unfamiliar people, she trusts her faerie more than me. And I have made it worse for her by staying distant. What can I do now to be the one she will rely on?*

Sorcha turned her head to stare at the doorway, growing pale once more. "They keep following me.

They beg me for songs. I don't know what their intentions are. What am I to do, Murdoch?"

"Well you can stay in the bath with me, for one," he said, an idea finally blooming in his mind.

She frowned. "And what will – how does that help me?"

Murdoch released his iron grip of her waist in order to trail his fingertips through the water; Sorcha followed the patterns they made with her eyes. "So long as there is no competition for a particular body of water," he explained, "a kelpie automatically claims dominion over it. The Unseelie cannot touch you in here."

When the water began to darken and swirl around them Sorcha gasped. "What are you doing? she asked, lifting a leg out of the water to see if the blackness had stained her skin. She carefully lowered it back in when she saw that it hadn't.

Murdoch let out a low chuckle. "I'm stretching myself out, so to speak. This was how I talked to you back in the waterfall pool, when I had to pretend to be Murdoch Buchanan whilst also meeting you as *me.*" He solidified a tendril of his very being and wrapped it around Sorcha's ankle, only to have it dissipate the moment she reached out a hand to try and touch it. "I sat by the water's edge and dipped my feet in it," Murdoch continued, "then toyed with you until you were almost out of breath."

Sorcha's eyes darted from one point in the bath to another, then another and another, never quite fast enough to catch sight of the next dark, twisting shape Murdoch hardened into being around her. "You enjoy toying with me," she murmured.

It wasn't a question.

Sorcha twisted her neck around until she could see Murdoch's expression. He let an amused smile cross his lips. "What do you expect me to say?" he asked. "Of course I enjoy it. Most all *otherwordly beings* like teasing humans. You are such easy targets."

"...you have hardly acted like this since you came to ask for your bridle back."

"That is because I have not had the means to act like this until now," Murdoch replied, indicating pointedly towards the water. "I can't make full use of my powers unless I'm in or near water."

Sorcha let out a bark of surprised laughter, though she held a hand over her mouth to try and cover the sound. "That is so obvious. I feel stupid for not realising that was the answer."

"I thought that was why you ran me the bath?" Murdoch asked, eyebrow raised. "Because you worked out I needed some time in water?"

"That was...p-part of the reason," she stammered, "but I thought it was more akin to being dehydrated than to you being cut off from your powers." A blush spread up Sorcha's neck, ears and cheeks, causing a stir somewhere below Murdoch's stomach, and he remembered that all that lay between himself and Sorcha's skin was her shirt. Feeling bold, and fuelled by lingering jealousy at her continued closeness to Lachlan and the insistent longing he'd held for her for years, Murdoch slid a hand beneath the hem of the garment to run his fingers against Sorcha's waist.

"For what other reason did you run me the bath then, Sorcha?" he murmured into her ear, thoroughly enjoying the resultant hitch in her breath at his question. "Were you hoping for something?"

"It d-doesn't matter," she stammered, trying to look away only to find Murdoch's other hand winding through her hair to keep her head in place. Murdoch allowed more of his body beneath the water to slide and dissolve and solidify again all around her until the artery in Sorcha's neck was throbbing painfully against his lips.

After two weeks of keeping his careful distance, Murdoch found every ounce of his resolve now evaporating as if it had never existed. He swept his hand further up Sorcha's body, delighting in the feeling of her squirming against him in response.

But not protesting. Not fighting to get away.

Murdoch grazed his lips along Sorcha's neck to the point where her jaw met her ear. "Do you want me to stop, Sorcha?" he breathed against her skin. "Do you want me to stop, or do you enjoy being toyed with as much as I enjoy doing it?"

Sorcha closed her eyes for a moment, lashes fluttering against her cheekbones as she shook her head. "I would not have run the bath if I wanted you to stop doing this," she said. "But..."

"But?"

Her gaze lingered on Murdoch's face. There was no mistaking the desire in her eyes; Murdoch felt a fool for ever believing it was truly gone.

Sorcha gulped. "Will you ever kiss me?" she whispered. "Or is torturing me all you want to do?"

"And what about you, Miss Darrow?" Murdoch bodily turned Sorcha around in his lap so that she was facing him. *For I have kissed you already,* he thought, *but you were enchanted. Why won't you kiss me first?*

Slowly but surely he worked his way through the buttons of her shirt until he reached her navel. Sorcha's breathing grew ever more uneven the lower his hands went. Murdoch watched her intently. "Will *you* ever kiss *me?*" he asked.

Sorcha blinked. She bit her lip. She breathed in through her nose. And then –

The two of them closed the gap between them simultaneously, Sorcha's hands crawling up Murdoch's neck to twist through his hair whilst he wrapped his arms around her waist to pull her closer, closer, closer. When their mouths found each other Murdoch leaned back to slide lower into the bath, pulling Sorcha with him. All around them the steaming water grew wild and turbulent, splashing over the edge of the tub to spill down onto the floor.

It can soak and stain the hallway carpet for all I care, Murdoch thought, dragging his lips away from Sorcha's to run hungry kisses down her neck. He wondered how he could have resisted putting her hands on her for as long as he had; now Sorcha was against his skin – in *his* environment – Murdoch didn't see how he could ever let her go.

He wanted her so badly. Loved her so much it was painful. It didn't matter that he currently despised Murdoch Buchanan; he would do anything to use the man's form to show Sorcha just how much he longed for her.

When Sorcha's hand grazed against Murdoch's hipbone it was his turn to gulp down a breath. He repositioned her in his lap, half a second away from flipping their positions so he could tower over her, when

The sound of porcelain smashing filled the air. Sorcha flinched; she broke away from Murdoch immediately, sitting stock straight in his lap in order to listen for further disturbances. "What was that?" she asked, eyes glued to the dark corridor through the doorway.

Murdoch tightened his grip on her, not ready for the magic woven around the two of them to break. "Mrs Ferguson probably had an accident –"

"I sent her to her room almost an hour ago," Sorcha interrupted. She placed a hand on Murdoch's shoulder to keep her balance as she stood up and exited the bath, further drenching the tiled floor as she did so. Murdoch watched her leave the bathroom, torn between leaping out to drag Sorcha back in to finish what they'd only just started and going to investigate alongside her.

Eventually his concern and curiosity got the better of him, and Murdoch lifted himself out of the bath. *We can talk about what we want to happen next after seeing what caused the noise,* he decided, wrapping a towel around his hips before following Sorcha into the shadowy corridor.

A tall, delicate vase that sat on the table near the hallway mirror had fallen to the floor. Heather, thistles and roses were scattered across the carpet alongside dangerously sharp fragments of porcelain. Sorcha stood in a dark puddle of water, eyes focused on a small, perfectly square card that she'd picked up with trembling hands.

"Sorcha?" Murdoch worried aloud, closing the distance between them in three broad strides. "Sorcha, what do you have in your –"

"*To the kelpie's bride,*" she said, voice taking on a sing-song lilt that disturbed Murdoch to no end, "*we suggest you choose your company a little more wisely in the days to come.*"

Murdoch grabbed onto Sorcha's arm to turn her around. Her eyes were glassy. "Where did you get that note?" he asked. "Do you recognise the handwriting?"

She shook her head, glanced at the table and said, "It was there. On the table. By the...by the mirror."

The mirror.

Murdoch stared at the reflective surface, trying desperately to see something within it that shouldn't have been there. But there was nothing.

It was just a mirror.

CHAPTER EIGHTEEN

Sorcha

Sorcha's head drooped over her cup of tea. The steam from the beverage caught in her lashes, making her eyes even heavier than they already were. So she closed them for just a moment, jolting herself back to reality when she realised she was beginning to doze in public.

Several days had passed since she had been given the Unseelie warning and Sorcha had barely slept. For how could she? There could be no mistaking that the note was a threat.

But for whom, exactly? Sorcha wondered for the hundredth time. *Me or Murdoch or Lachlan? They called me the kelpie's bride, but did not specify that it was* his *company I should be wary about. It could well be Lachlan's, since he is the Seelie king. Or it could be somebody else's company entirely.*

She sighed heavily, fighting the insatiable urge to rest her head upon the table and block out the rest of the world. On Murdoch's orders, Mrs Ferguson had taken Sorcha to a coffee house near the Grey and MacKinnon offices in Mayfair whilst he attended a meeting.

"Miss Darrow, are you quite all right?" Mrs Ferguson asked, a frown of worry creasing her brow. She held a hand to Sorcha's forehead. "You seem to have a chill."

"I am just tired, Mrs Ferguson," Sorcha replied, which was at the very least a half-truth. She blew upon the surface of her tea. "Do you think Mr Buchanan will be much longer?"

"I imagine he should be here any moment. I must confess, I am most pleased that Mr Buchanan has finally settled down. His father would be very happy if he were around to see it."

Finally settled down? Sorcha wondered. *If his own housekeeper is saying such a thing then he truly must have been quite a Lothario. I always thought the kelpie was exaggerating when he told me that two years ago.*

But it did not matter how Murdoch Buchanan acted around women one way or the other. The man was dead, and the creature who had replaced him only had eyes for Sorcha.

Or at least I think that must be true, she mused, hating how conflicted she still felt over the subject. After their altercation in the bath Sorcha had thought that perhaps she and the kelpie would end up on more of an even keel with each other, and though Murdoch had not reverted to silence after the note from the Unseelie there was still something distinctly careful about the way he talked and acted around Sorcha in the days that followed.

He was never so conflicted two years ago. Even when

he was pretending to be someone else I never doubted his interest in me. What has him so distracted now? Does he mislike bearing a human form for so long?

It would not surprise Sorcha if she were to discover that this was the case, but it hurt her heart to believe such a thing. For if the kelpie could only stand to be human for a short duration of time then it would not matter if she sorted out how she felt for him; their relationship would be doomed from the beginning.

Even if I were immortal things would not change, Sorcha thought, taking a long draught of her quickly-cooling tea as she did so. *I would still be no more magical than I am now.*

Sorcha had been mulling over Lachlan's not-so-subtle wishes that she accept his offer to live in the Seelie Court amongst the faeries for a long time now. Though she loved her home, and wished to protect the land around the loch as had always been the Darrow tradition, Sorcha had to admit that the allure of a human life was waning.

My father is not long for this world, and my mother may not be far behind for all I know. When they are gone, who else ties me to this life?

But, even taking that into account, over the past two years Sorcha had still staunchly refused Lachlan's offer. For she *was* human, and this was her life. It felt as if she would be running away from her responsibilities if she left the human realm.

That was before she received the note from the Unseelie.

Now all Sorcha could think about was whether she would be safer becoming immortal and living under the protection of the Seelie Court. It seemed like her best course of action. But then...

Sorcha sighed once more. It was folly for her to think such a solution was her best option. She was human and forever was a long, long time. Even after her parents were gone she would have decades to live. Sorcha had to carve a life out for *herself,* instead of relying on Lachlan and Ailith and their otherworldly magic.

When she heard the bell above the coffee house door ring Sorcha glanced over at the entrance. A man and a woman dressed in long, vibrant-coloured cloaks headed to the counter, a paper-wrapped package held firmly in the woman's hands. Their hoods were pulled high over their heads so Sorcha could not see what they looked like, but as they spoke Sorcha realised they both had distinctly German accents.

"Not often we get foreigners here," Mrs Ferguson said, eyeing the couple curiously. "Their clothes are expensive, though. They must be important."

Whilst the woman dealt with the coffee house owner, giving the man hushed instructions that were clearly to do with the package in her hands, her companion wandered around the shop until he spotted Sorcha, locking his gaze on her as if he had been searching for her. She was startled into sitting stock straight, for his eyes were almost as golden as Lachlan's.

Amber, she realised. *Not gold. Is he a faerie?*

The man cocked his head to one side as he regarded Sorcha. She fidgeted with her tea cup, wondering what on earth to say to him when he finally broke the silence instead. "What strange eyes you have," he murmured, frowning slightly. Sorcha distinctly felt like he was staring right through her. She wanted to look away, but forced herself to match the man's stare.

"Not as strange as yours, perhaps," she said – a comment which was bold enough to elicit a gasp of shock from Mrs Ferguson. But Sorcha did not care if the servant thought her rude; if the man was at all offended then it was his own fault for talking to Sorcha first.

The stranger's frown grew deeper, though it seemed altogether more out of concern than offence. "Be careful so far from home," he warned Sorcha. "Be very careful." He retreated back to his companion's side just as Murdoch opened the door to the coffee house and strode right on past him; his unsettling eyes peered at the kelpie in disguise as if he were confused. "But...not of him," the man said, so quietly Sorcha almost missed it.

Murdoch glanced at the stranger, wariness and suspicion apparent on his face, before sitting down to join Sorcha and Mrs Ferguson. "Do you know him, Miss Darrow?" he asked, firing another look behind him as he spoke.

It took Sorcha a long moment before she shook her head. The amber-eyed man's words struck a chord with her, especially after the Unseelie warning. *Just who is he?* she wondered, curious and just a little bit frightened.

"You attract the most bizarre folk," Murdoch said, stealing a bite of Sorcha's untouched lemon cake much to the distress of a scandalised Mrs Ferguson. Sorcha held his gaze, fighting the urge to smile. For wasn't Murdoch the most bizarre creature of all that Sorcha had attracted?

"How did your meeting go?" she asked, quickly

changing the subject. "Have you made any headway?"

Murdoch's face darkened immediately. "They are most insistent that they want this land. We have been invited to a private art viewing by Mr MacKinnon this Saturday, and I have a feeling they will use the opportunity to attempt to corral you into signing it over to them directly."

Sorcha mulled this over for a minute. She did not much like the idea of being *corralled* into anything, but she could stand to stay trapped in Mr Buchanan's house for another few days even less.

"Let us go," she said, "and they will see just how foolish they are to think they can convince *me* to do something I do not wish to do."

Murdoch raised an eyebrow. "You wouldn't be thinking of escaping through a window, would you?"

"That depends – would you follow me?"

A knowing smile crossed his face. "You did say you would be difficult, two years ago. But I do recall telling you that I was willing to put the effort in, regardless."

"Is that a yes?" Sorcha asked, heart thumping so painfully in her chest that she thought it might stop. She wished she and Murdoch were alone and in private. But they were not, which meant so much could not be said.

Murdoch's black eyes glittered with the promise of something Sorcha was desperate to explore again. "I suppose it is," he said, before sweeping back onto his feet. "Now, come; it is time we went home."

Sorcha wished the kelpie meant Darach. Going by the look on his face, so did he.

CHAPTER NINETEEN

Murdoch

"Mister Buchanan, are you listening to me?"

"Probably not; he's too busy pretending not to stare at his betrothed."

Murdoch bit his tongue in surprise at having been caught out, for he was indeed not listening to the conversation his colleagues were having in favour of watching Sorcha. She was milling from painting to painting, taking note of the artist's name and the year the painting was completed before scanning each piece from top to bottom, searching for...something.

I want to ask her what she's thinking when she looks at each painting, Murdoch pined, curling his hands into fists at his side for but a moment before relaxing them again. Things had been incredibly tense ever since the Unseelie left their note of warning for Sorcha. Given that they had referred to her as 'the kelpie's bride' Murdoch could only run on the assumption that the dark fae were following her because of him.

Because he murdered the Unseelie king's brother and nephew.

That was never supposed to hurt Sorcha, he thought, glancing wistfully at her as she twirled her cream dress around her feet and headed to look at an ancient Egyptian vessel. Gregory MacKinnon's art collection was admittedly impressive but the wing of his estate which housed said collection was far too ostentatious for Murdoch's liking. There was a lot of gold, for one, which reminded Murdoch too much of Lachlan's palace for his comfort. *And too many reflective surfaces through which the Unseelie could reach out to Sorcha.*

"Mister Buchanan, you are seriously distracted."

"To be distracted by my betrothed seems like a blessing, given I shall be spending the rest of my life with her," Murdoch replied, altogether rather wry. It was difficult for him *not* to make a joke of anything pertaining to Mr Buchanan still being alive.

Gregory let out a decidedly cruel laugh; there was a sneer on his face that Murdoch did not like at all. "Given your behaviour in the past, I somehow doubt Miss Darrow will hold your attention for as long as you think she will. I doubt any woman would, no matter how charming."

Murdoch resisted responding. From combing through Mr Buchanan's memories he had come to discover just how free with his affections the man had been whilst living in London. He had ventured up to visit William Darrow with no intention whatsoever of staying true to Sorcha, though his glib charm and lingering fondness for the area that used to be his home had won her father over and concealed his ultimate goal for seeking her hand.

He was useful, in order to meet her, Murdoch thought. *And he was supposed to be useful now, but he has become such a burden to me.*

"Speaking of Miss Darrow," Howard Grey chimed in, a mischievous look creasing the lines around his eyes, "have you broached the subject of a winter wedding to her yet? The ball is just around the corner, Murdoch! You are running out of time to ask her."

"I do not think it fair to spring such a thing on her," Murdoch replied. "She has always wanted to get married by the loch-side." He scratched his chin and pretended to be thoughtful as he lied, for in truth Murdoch was fairly certain Sorcha did not wish to get married at all.

No marriage to a mere mortal could best a relationship with a faerie king, he thought, though Murdoch hated acknowledging Lachlan as one of Sorcha's suitors at all. But what Ailith had said to him still rang in his head – that the Seelie king had offered Sorcha the world. Murdoch wondered what *the world* entailed, for it wasn't as if Sorcha spoke to him about her thoughts on the faerie.

She was always guarded when it came to Lachlan.

"One wonders if you are delaying the proceedings deliberately," Gregory remarked, forcing Murdoch out of his own head once more. "If you truly love Miss Darrow then why do you seem so reluctant to marry her?"

Murdoch knew this was as good an opportunity as any to say that he did not wish to hand over the Darrow land to Grey and MacKinnon, and hope that their respect and friendship with Mr Buchanan would prevent them from using much more underhanded techniques to procure it. After a handful of meetings with the board he had found no way to convince them that their plan was a bad one, which left Murdoch with no choice but to go down the personal route.

He turned to the two men, making himself as tall and imposing as possible. "After having spent the last fortnight in London I must confess that the city has lost its charm for me," he began. From the looks on the faces of both Howard and Gregory they could already tell where this was going – and did not like it. Murdoch continued on anyway. "I have enjoyed my life back by Loch Lomond these past two years. I do not wish to see it end."

"There would be no need for that to change," Howard said. "From the money we make from Miss Darrow's land we will all be very, very wealthy men. You could retire early wherever you wanted!"

"I do not see how Miss Darrow would ever forgive me if I sold her home to investors the moment we wed. It is the one thing she and her family do not want, and I would be loathe to betray her like that."

"You –" Gregory spluttered, his pale face slowly turning scarlet. "I knew you were not right for this job! I should have sent my son and been done with it!"

Howard did not seem as visibly angry, though there was a tightness to his eyes that had not been there before. He wagged his glass of port at Murdoch. "Now, now, Murdoch," he said, as if he were scorning a child, "you cannot back out of this now. You were *paid* to do this, and handsomely. Do not turn away from a promising career with people who respect you over a lowly country girl!"

"The problem is that I do not respect *you*," Murdoch countered, seething with anger on Sorcha's behalf. "Anybody who would tear apart such a beautiful area of the country for money – upending the lives of hundreds of honest-working families in the process – deserves the respect of no-one. Good evening."

And with that Murdoch stormed away from his colleagues, knowing that he was bound to pay dearly for having spoken to them the way he had. *If they try to take the land by force I shall kill them all,* he thought, a shiver of wicked excitement tingling his spine. *I have spent too long as someone else. It is time I fight for my home as myself. For* our *home,* Murdoch added on, making a beeline for Sorcha.

He had wasted so much time hating the vessel he was in. Precious time. Time Murdoch should have been spending with the woman he loved.

Sorcha turned from the painting she was looking at as if she could tell Murdoch was making his way to her. A radiant smile lit up her face, and she tucked a stray lock of hair behind her ear. But just as she opened her mouth to greet him, a hand on Murdoch's arm tugged him away.

His eyes flashed a warning as he looked to see who had touched him, but it was merely a blonde-haired woman around Sorcha's age. "Mister Buchanan?" she said, a little unsure, and then, brightly, "Oh, it *is* you! It has been so long!"

"Oh my goodness, you have gotten even more handsome since last I saw you," another woman agreed when she joined the first. Murdoch cast a furtive glance at Sorcha, whose eyes narrowed at the scene in front of her. He did not like that at all. "How long has it been?" the woman continued. "Two, three years?"

Murdoch did not know what to say. He vaguely

recognised the two women from Mr Buchanan's memories – casual dalliances from the man's past. "Whilst it is wonderful to see the two of you," he said, forcing a smile to his face, "it is with regret I must inform you that I am on my way out. I was just about to fetch – Miss Darrow?"

He searched over the heads of the women, but Murdoch could not see Sorcha. He felt like pulling his hair out. *Just once I wish things could be easy between us,* he raged, walking away from the two women without so much as a goodbye. *Why must there always be faerie usurpers and fox curses and golden princes and greedy, filthy Londoners to contend with?*

"And your hedonistic, awful past," Murdoch glowered at his reflection when he passed a vase encased in glass. "This is your fault. Yours."

He did not want to admit that, had he been more open and honest with Sorcha from the beginning, Murdoch may well have avoided this situation entirely.

Being a human is terrible.

CHAPTER TWENTY

Sorcha

I guess Murdoch Buchanan really was the Lothario the kelpie warned me about.

Sorcha couldn't stand to watch it.

"This is so stupid," she muttered, snaking around all the well-dressed people who had come to bear witness to Gregory MacKinnon's new art collection in her attempt to escape the sight of Murdoch surrounded by pretty, English socialites. Mister MacKinnon had come to procure a few paintings that Sorcha was familiar with – works by Scottish artists whom her mother and father knew – and many of the guests stood idolising the bleak, Scottish landscapes captured on the canvas, describing them as *romantic* and *heartbreakingly beautiful*.

They do not get to think that if they do not live there, she grumbled, growing more and more frustrated with everyone around her. *You cannot appreciate the Scottish wilderness if you have not also suffered through its stormy autumns and tempestuous winters.*

Sorcha knew she couldn't exactly blame anyone for adoring the paintings, for they *were* beautiful. But there was a heavy, leaden pit within her, gnawing away at her nerves and leaving her feeling raw and exposed. Sorcha had thought attending the art exhibit would have allowed her and Murdoch to at least spend some time together as a couple, even if their engagement was false. She'd hoped it would encourage them to talk about how they actually felt for each other.

Instead, Murdoch had spent most of the evening embroiled with his colleagues and then surrounded by lovely-looking, fawning women. Sorcha did not think she had ever been jealous before – not even of Ailith, who was perfect in every way a creature could be perfect. But she was jealous now, and she hated it.

Why is it that the only one who does not get to spend time with Murdoch is me? I am the only one who truly knows him. All the people around me are chasing a ghost.

As she always did, Sorcha pushed the man's death to the back of her mind. There was nothing she could do about the fact the kelpie had devoured him and, considering how Mr Buchanan had intended to trick her into handing over the Darrow land, Sorcha had to admit that part of her was glad that he had died.

If that makes me a terrible person then so be it. Given the otherworldy nature of the folk I consider my friends, I have not been all that great at being human for a while.

Something about that made Sorcha feel wildly uncomfortable. Was she beginning to lose sight of who she was? Had she spent too long in London with a terrifying, powerful beast masquerading as a man for her own good? For when the two of them had been in the bath – when the kelpie had been more like himself than he had been since Sorcha stole away his bridle – Murdoch *had* been terrifying. He'd been full of the same dark intensity that had caused Sorcha to run from him the very first night she met him.

But it was that darkness that kept drawing Sorcha to him, too. That made her want and desire him; that made her wish dearly to *know* him.

London, and the people within it, were preventing her from doing so.

"I want to go home," she wailed, so softly that she was sure nobody could hear her.

Somebody did.

"I had a feeling London was not to your tastes, lass," a man said from over on her left, his voice so light and airy that Sorcha thought for a moment she had imagined it. She turned to face him, taking a step back in surprise when she noticed there was something familiar about him.

The man was tall and lithe, dressed in a resplendent, elaborately-embroidered tailcoat the colour of deep, dark wine. He inclined his head politely at Sorcha, a spirited smile lighting up his fine features. Though he had long, silver hair kept tied away from his face, the man seemed to be no more than a year or two older than Murdoch Buchanan.

And then Sorcha realised why she thought he seemed familiar.

Silver hair.

"We have met before," she said carefully. "You helped me find my way when I was lost."

135

"Consider me a concerned third party looking out for your welfare," he said, grey eyes glittering as they swept from Sorcha's head to her feet. She blushed and looked away.

"I believed you to be an old man, truth be told," she admitted.

He laughed easily and ran a hand across his temple. "Because of my hair?"

Sorcha nodded. "Your face was covered, too, so I did not see it. But you are not so old."

"How generous of you to say so. Might you accompany me whilst I take a turn around this exhibit?" The man proffered an arm and Sorcha, before she knew what she was doing, took it. When he guided her down the corridor it almost felt as if they were gliding across the marble rather than walking. Sorcha had not felt such ease in moving since she had travelled down to London on the back of a kelpie.

Murdoch, Sorcha remembered, coming back to her senses in a moment of clarity. *Where is he?*

"It seems as if your companion is otherwise occupied," the silver-haired man said, glancing at Sorcha out of the corner of his eye. "The tall, dark, brooding gentleman who was surrounded by ladies, yes?"

Sorcha did not respond, though her silence was more than enough of an answer.

"Is he part of the reason you wish to leave London?" he ventured, taking two glasses of wine from a passing servant and handing one to Sorcha. She accepted the glass but did not drink from it, wary as she was, choosing instead to concentrate on looking at the paintings they passed as they walked.

"He is and he is not," she said, which was the truth. It was because of the kelpie that she wanted to go home; it was because of *Murdoch Buchanan* that she did not wish to stay in London.

"A perfectly evasive answer, Miss Darrow."

A terribly foreboding shiver ran down Sorcha's spine. She dared not look at the man as she asked, "How do you know my name?"

"If I could lie, I would say I learned it from your Mr Buchanan's colleagues. But he is no more a man than I am, Miss Darrow, and you need to be careful. Kelpies are dark, dangerous creatures, and this one in particular even more so. You did receive my note, did you not?"

He is Unseelie, Sorcha realised, so shocked she could barely process anything but this one, all-consuming fact. *He is Unseelie. He is –*

"Oh, I am not here to harm you," the faerie said, laughing his light, disarming laugh again. Sorcha risked a glance at him; he was staring at her with a highly curious expression painting his angular features. "I am merely here to pose a question to you. I was hoping you would be so kind as to answer it."

"I...I suppose it would depend on the question," Sorcha replied, very slowly. She hardly felt able to wrap her mouth around the words she said; they felt thick and foreign on her tongue.

The mysterious stranger came to a stop and took a long draught from his wine; when he pulled the glass away his lips were stained a purple just as deep as his tailcoat. It unsettled Sorcha greatly, especially when the faerie leaned towards her, boxing her in against the wall.

"Tell me," he began, "why do you continue to

decline the Seelie king's most generous offer of immortality?"

"What did you just say?"

Sorcha froze, for she had not asked the question.

It was Murdoch.

CHAPTER TWENTY-ONE

Murdoch

"You turned down *what?*"

Sorcha's eyes widened in shock as she turned her head to stare at Murdoch. A tall, silver-haired man was looming over her, dangerously close to her face, but in the space of a blink he disappeared.

A faerie. Which is why he knew about the offer of immortality.

Sorcha's head swung around wildly when she realised the person she'd been speaking to was gone. Her skin was pale, and the wine glass in her hand was shaking. "Murdoch, I never meant to keep it from –"

"*Why were you talking to an Unseelie?*" he demanded, too furious with the immediate issue at hand to focus on what the faerie himself had said. He stalked towards Sorcha, grabbed her sleeve and dragged her towards the nearest exit, not caring if anybody could see them. The two of them had to leave London *now,* before their situation grew worse than it already was.

"Murdoch, stop – stop pulling me along!" Sorcha cried out the moment they hit the bracing night air. She scrabbled at his hand, digging in her nails until he let her go. "I did not know he was Unseelie when he started talking to me!"

"And yet you followed him down an empty corridor and allowed him to corner you like a cat with a mouse. Have you listened to nothing either myself or Lachlan has warned you about? Have you?"

Sorcha glowered at him. She ran her hands up and down her arms, for in Murdoch's haste to leave Gregory MacKinnon's abode he had left their coats and scarves back inside. "There would have been no opportunity for me to be cornered if you hadn't been so *occupied,* Mister Buchanan."

Murdoch recoiled as if Sorcha had slapped him. "You know that was not me they were wishing to talk to," he said, hating the scathing look in her eyes before she turned her back on him. "Sorcha, you cannot blame me for –"

"I know I cannot blame you!" she cut in. Her hands curled into small, angry fists at her sides, entire back shivering from either fury or cold. Murdoch reasoned that it was likely both. "I cannot blame you for what Mr Buchanan was like in the past," Sorcha continued, "but that does not mean I like it, nor the way you – you –"

"Nor the way I *what,* Sorcha?"

"It does not matter," she sniffed.

Murdoch reached out a hand to touch her arm but Sorcha pulled away. "I will get our coats," he said, trying desperately to calm his temper even though he was still viciously angry. But he was not angry *with* Sorcha. He was, however, confused and hurt because of her. *She did not once tell me Lachlan offered her immortality,* Murdoch thought as he jogged back to the front door, where a servant was dutifully waiting with his and Sorcha's outerwear. He thanked the man, wasting no time in throwing on his coat before turning back the way he had come, and froze.

Sorcha had disappeared into the night.

"Do not do this now, Sorcha!" Murdoch called out, hating the way his voice shook as he shouted. It felt as if bile was rising in his throat; every time he turned away from Sorcha for even a moment she seemed to get into trouble.

Going by the appearance of the Unseelie tonight, she was running out of opportunities to escape said trouble unscathed.

"Sorcha," Murdoch said into the night, gentler this time as he crunched across gravel and reached the elaborately-designed, wrought-iron front gates of the MacKinnon estate. "Sorcha, please. You know this is dangerous. Let us return home and *talk*. We have not done nearly enough of that. Sorcha? Sorcha!"

His heart beat erratically in his chest when he realised the front gates had not been opened, which meant Sorcha hadn't left the dark, expansive grounds of the estate. *Just where have you gone, you fool?* Murdoch thought as he ran across a stretch of frost-covered grass, slipping more than once and just barely regaining his balance before he fell over each time. He searched around for something – anything.

And then he saw it: footprints.

Footprints that matched the slippers Sorcha had

been wearing, heading towards a glassy, largely frozen-over ornamental pond. It was a rather enormous body of water, more akin to a lake now that Murdoch was growing nearer to it, but all around its frosted edges Sorcha was nowhere to be seen.

"Where *are* you, Sorcha?!" Murdoch boomed, voice echoing all around. But then he noticed a fault in the ice upon the water, as if someone had come across a crack and fallen straight down.

Murdoch's heart stopped beating for one sick, terrible moment.

He dived into the lake without a second thought, reverting to his true form the moment the water's surface settled above him. Shards of ice filtered through the inky-black water; what little light Murdoch could make out with his keen eyes reflected off their sharp edges, turning them into silvered knives. He kicked at the long, tumbling weeds growing from the bottom of the lake the moment they touched him, all the while searching, searching, searching for anything even vaguely human-shaped.

"Sorcha," he whispered, the water carrying his voice to the farthest corners of the lake as if he had screamed. "Sorcha," he said again, "where are you?"

C-cold, came a faint, stuttering reply. Murdoch swung immediately to his right, dissolving into the water to hurtle through it as fast as he could. *Caught on something. C-can't breathe.*

"Just hold on!" he cried, growing desperate when he still could not locate Sorcha. "Call out again! Tell me where you are!"

Slipped, Sorcha thought. *So s-stupid. I am so stupid.*

"You are a fool, but you are not stupid," Murdoch replied. He had to keep Sorcha thinking – had to ensure her brain continued to function until he found and freed her. He scanned the bottom of the lake, fighting with the strangling weeds for a sight of a hand or a foot or the hem of a dress, and then –

A long, flowing tendril that was not a weed glinted in a stray sliver of moonlight, flashing deep copper against the murky water.

"Found you!" Murdoch roared, relief washing over him as he galloped through the lake to reach Sorcha. Several weeds had wound themselves around her legs; he tore at them with vicious, frantic teeth until Sorcha, finally, floated free.

Her eyes were closed, her face ghostly pale. Murdoch could tell Sorcha was no longer breathing.

"Don't you dare die!" he screamed, forcing Sorcha onto his back until her hands brushed against his bridle, filling her with the power to breathe and stay attached to Murdoch. *Don't you dare die like this. You cannot drown. It is impossible.*

But as Murdoch hurtled away from the lake and through the streets of London back to Mr Buchanan's house, his thoughts from before kept circling in his head. Perhaps Sorcha really *had* run out of opportunities to escape from danger – but not at the hands of the Unseelie. No, they may well have been the ones who were correct, after all. She should have chosen her company a little more wisely.

If she'd never dallied with a kelpie then Sorcha Darrow would not have found herself drowning in that lake.

CHAPTER TWENTY-TWO

Sorcha

All around Sorcha was cold, cold, cold, so bitter and biting that her skin felt like it was burning or had been stabbed with a million tiny needles. Her lungs gasped for air, but when she opened her mouth she was greeted with a torrent of ice water, instead. She could not move her legs; could not kick away from whatever was trapping her beneath the surface of the lake.

I am going to die, Sorcha thought, so deliriously oxygen-deprived that she did not notice the way the water around her solidified just before she closed her eyes. Then everything went black, and Sorcha knew she would never again wake up.

*

"...cha. Sorcha. Sorcha, please, you must wake up!"

A flicker of warmth went through her, growing stronger with every passing second. Eventually that heat was all Sorcha could feel, and the darkness around her abated a little.

She opened her eyes.

Murdoch was looming over her, unfocused at first until she blinked a few times. His face was pale and terrified and wretched; the whites of his eyes were red and bleary, as if he had been crying. Sorcha realised she was lying on the floor of his bedroom by the fire, and several blankets were wrapped around her body. Out of the corner of her eye Sorcha spotted her sodden clothes abandoned by the door.

I really did – I almost drowned. I almost died. All because I threw a childish tantrum.

Sorcha coughed and spluttered as she tried to sit up. Her chest was in agony; she clutched her hands to it and heaved.

Murdoch placed firm but gentle hands on her shoulders to push her back to the floor. "Don't get up," he soothed. "Just stay where you are for a while. You are frozen through."

Now that Sorcha was becoming aware of her own body she realised that Murdoch was right. Every inch of her skin prickled and stung with the cold, and the fire hurt equally as much as it thawed her out. "S-sorry," she apologised through chattering teeth. She could hardly stand to look at Murdoch, she felt so miserably guilty. "I'm s–"

"I know you are. I know you are, but I should have expected something like this to happen."

Sorcha frowned, and peered at Murdoch through the dim, crackling light of the fire. "What do you mean?"

"You are the girl who flees through windows into the dead of night," he laughed bitterly, leaning against the hearth and closing his eyes to the heat. Murdoch had stripped down to his shirt and breeches, which were both dripping wet. They steamed faintly as the fire dried them out. "I should have known it was only a matter of time before you ran from me again."

Sorcha gulped on a throat full of tears. "That wasn't – I didn't – I was *angry*, Murdoch, and I –"

"You almost *died*, Sorcha!" Murdoch bit out. She realised he *was* crying; a trail of moisture down his cheek glinted in the fire light. "You almost died, because of me. The Unseelie warned you about being in my company and they were *right*."

With tremendous effort Sorcha forced herself into a sitting position. Her hair hung in cold, wet tendrils around her face, so she ran a shaking hand through it all to push it back. She edged out a foot to touch Murdoch's knee, desperately wanting him to open his eyes and look at her.

"You would never hurt me," Sorcha said, very softly. "You said so yourself. I have always trusted you, Murdoch."

"But it is my actions against others that are putting you in danger. I am a kelpie who has waged war against the faerie realm. You should never have been put in the middle of it."

Sorcha said nothing. She knew Murdoch was right, in some respects, but it had always been her choice to get involved with both the kelpie and the Seelie. If anyone was to blame for Sorcha being in danger then it was herself.

Especially tonight.

Neither of them spoke for a while, Sorcha staring at

Murdoch whilst he kept his eyes closed as they both warmed their frozen bodies by the fire. Eventually Sorcha stopped shaking, and her nerves stopped hurting, and the blankets wrapped around her grew uncomfortably hot.

She pulled them off until all but one silken cover remained.

"You will get cold again, Sorcha," Murdoch mumbled. She realised he was watching her beneath barely-open, heavy-hooded eyes; she blushed profusely.

"I am too hot now," she said. "The blankets were sticking to my skin. Your wet clothes most be uncomfortable, too."

Murdoch glanced down at his shirt, causing Sorcha's eyes to wander with his. The material was clinging to every plane of his body, as were his breeches. She looked away before her imagination could run rampant.

"I suppose you are right," he replied, pulling off his shirt with a wince when the wet material brushed past his face. Murdoch threw it into some dark corner of the room, then grabbed for one of Sorcha's abandoned blankets to cover him from the waist down so he could remove the rest of his clothes, too.

Sorcha giggled despite herself. "I never knew kelpies were so modest."

"I'd rather say that it is *your* immodesty that is strange here," he countered. "I have never known a human to have such blatant disregard for her own privacy. You stripped off all your clothes in front of me back when you swam in the waterfall pool, though you still believed me to be a man!"

"That was because I wanted to," Sorcha replied,

arching her back until she felt a satisfying pop in her upper spine.

"You wanted to?"

"Well, considering what had almost happened the night before in my tent –"

"So you wanted to continue on from where Lachlan had so rudely interrupted us?" Murdoch asked, dark eyes intent on Sorcha's. He leaned towards her just a little. "Because as I recall, you went to the waterfall pool to try and talk to the kelpie, not seduce a man."

"I...may have wanted both," Sorcha admitted, turning her gaze to the fire out of sheer embarrassment. Her body was still burning, though the source of the heat was entirely internal. "I did not understand it at the time, but once I discovered who you were – who Murdoch Buchanan was – it finally made sense to me."

"So it was not the man himself who you were attracted to?"

"Oh, lord no!" Sorcha cried out, putting her hands up in protest in front of her chest. She glanced at Murdoch; a somewhat confused look was plastered to his handsome face. "I mean," she corrected, "of course he is...good to look at. But I could never have been attracted to the real man. Tonight only further solidified that point."

"Tonight did?"

"You had no time for me at the exhibit," Sorcha explained. "It was all about work and being distracted by other women. I...could never put up with that. It was infuriating."

The smallest of smiles quirked Murdoch's lips. "You were *jealous,* Sorcha?"

148

"...yes."

And then, out of nowhere, Murdoch threw his head back and burst out laughing. It was hearty and genuine – a sound Sorcha had not heard in two years. She ached for it. "You are – you have nothing to be jealous of, Miss Darrow," he said, still laughing. "You know I only have eyes for you."

"So why have you been so distant these past three weeks?"

Sorcha moved forward on her knees, barely covering herself with the silk blanket as she closed the gap between herself and Murdoch. He watched her every move like a hawk, all humour lost from his face in an instant.

"Because I hate him," Murdoch replied, very quietly. "Mister Buchanan, that is. I cannot stand him. Down here, in London, it has been harder and harder for me to split myself from the man I look like. I did not want to be near you when I felt this way."

"I do not see him when I look at you." Sorcha moved even closer to Murdoch, until it was the easiest thing in the world to reach out a hand to stroke her fingers along the planes of his face. His eyes burned like coals as she traced a line across his cheekbones and down his jaw. "I have never seen him," she continued, "I have only seen you. How could you not know that?"

When Murdoch took hold of her hand and placed it over his heart Sorcha gasped in surprise. "Because I am so nervous I think I might be sick," he admitted, pressing her hand even further against his chest until all Sorcha could feel was an erratic, throbbing pulse from behind his ribs. "I have been like this ever since I knocked upon your door and begged for your help. I forced you to choose sides, two years ago, and you chose the faeries. You chose Lachlan. I thought –"

"I did not *choose* Lachlan over you," Sorcha scolded. "If it were as easy as that I would have stolen away your bridle the moment you fell asleep. But I couldn't. Even when we were up on the plinth and you were drowning everyone in sight I struggled to do what needed to be done. But the fight I was put in the middle of...it was bigger than me. I could not let anyone suffer if I could stop it, even if the last thing I wanted to do was betray you."

Murdoch's eyes widened. He slid a hand over Sorcha's. "You did not betray me. You –"

"I did. But it was the right thing to do, though it tortured me to think about it after you were banished to the loch. Murdoch...you have no idea how much I missed you, after you were gone."

A flash of desire crossed his face; in the mirror of the kelpie's dark, fathomless eyes Sorcha could see the same desire on her own face, too. His grip tightened on her hand. "Why did you refuse Lachlan's offer of immortality?"

Sorcha bit her lip. *How do I make an immortal being understand when I barely understand it myself?* She looked down at their entwined hands. "Because I am human," she said eventually, "and I would rather carve out a meaningful life of sixty years – a life where I feel everything – than live forever and grow numb to the world. I –"

Murdoch kissed her, very softly. "Then let's feel something," he murmured, the words dancing on Sorcha's lips. He snaked a tightly-muscled arm around her, easily flipping their positions so that Sorcha's back was to the wall with Murdoch pressed against her.

Sorcha slid a hand through his hair, still sodden and cold from the lake beneath her fingertips. She ran kisses down Murdoch's neck the way he'd done to her in the bath and, two years ago, in her tent, digging her teeth in when she reached his shoulder. Murdoch groaned at the sensation, and he pulled at Sorcha's thighs to wrap them around his waist.

"Was that a yes?" he asked, voice low and dark and full of longing against Sorcha's ear.

And there it was – the terrifying thrill Sorcha had been longing for from the very first moment she met the kelpie. An inexorable hook that pulled her towards him even as the creature's sheer power loomed all around, reminding Sorcha that he could – and did – kill without a second thought.

But not her. Never her.

"That was a yes," she said, tightening her arms around Murdoch's neck and crushing her lips to his. "It was always a yes."

CHAPTER TWENTY-THREE

Murdoch

The first time Murdoch witnessed Sorcha Margaret Darrow sleeping she had been three years old.

Her parents had taken her down to the shore in front of their house, letting their little girl play in the shallow end of the loch to her heart's content beneath the high-summer son. It had been very hot that year, even for July, so the family of three had lingered by the water's edge for much of the day.

Little Sorcha had played for hours and hours before tiring herself out. She sprawled out across the wet sand, fingers of her right hand just barely touching the loch, and sang along inexpertly to the melody her mother was whistling. Sorcha giggled when the water began swirling around her hand, moving in a way that seemed impossible. But she was three, and exhausted, so she did not think anything of it at the time.

Murdoch had made sure to check in on her every summer since then, delighted with how much time she spent in and around Loch Lomond. It was his home but it was hers, too, and it was clear that she adored it.

He would have done anything to protect her from harm.

And so it was that the kelpie of Loch Lomond had never imagined he would find himself lying in bed with that same mortal girl, now a full-fledged woman, in the form of a human himself. When Murdoch had first taken on Mr Buchanan's form he'd thought to take advantage of it simply to meet Sorcha – to talk with her in her house and perhaps gather more information on Grey and MacKinnon's plans for the Darrow land in the process.

It should not have surprised him that he merely fell for Sorcha even more. Murdoch knew it would not be possible to return to the loch without getting to spend more time with her. And the vessel he was using was going to *marry* her. It had seemed all too fortuitous.

But then Sorcha had fled out of her bedroom window, and dallied with a fox who was a faerie prince. Murdoch had thought things to be ruined between them before they had even started, but then Sorcha had sought out a kelpie.

She had sought out *him*.

And though so much had happened since then, and Sorcha had broken Murdoch's heart as easily as she'd snapped off his bridle, somehow the two of them were together now. They were together, and they were happy in each other's arms, and soon they would be home, too. Which meant there was just one, lingering problem.

Lachlan's offer of immortality.

"Mister Buchanan?" Mrs Ferguson called through

his bedroom door, knocking gently as she did so. "You have a letter from the office. It seems as if it may be urgent."

Murdoch stroked Sorcha's hair, revelling in the sound of her soft breathing and the rosy colouring of her cheeks. She was completely, wondrously at ease, a word that had not once described her in the three weeks since Murdoch had shown up at her door begging for his bridle back.

He slid out of bed, throwing on a robe before answering the door to receive the letter from Mrs Ferguson. The flicker of a smile crossed her face at her employer's unkempt appearance, though she quickly schooled her expression back to neutral.

"Would you like some breakfast?" she asked. "It is almost ten."

But Murdoch shook his head. "We are fine for now, Mrs Ferguson. In fact, take the day off if you like. We will be quite content on our own."

The woman wordlessly receded as Murdoch closed the door and ripped open the envelope in his hands. He recognised the handwriting as that of Gregory MacKinnon's; he wondered if it was an official notice of his termination from the company. Murdoch sat down upon his bed as softly as he could so as not to rouse Sorcha from her sleep, unfurling the letter with a sense of grim satisfaction.

Dear Mr Buchanan, it read;

We at Grey and MacKinnon sincerely apologise for the manner in which the Darrow land was discussed at my abode. I am sorry in particular for the way I personally acted. We understand now that the land is more important to your future family than we gave it credit for.

As a gesture of our continued friendship, please do consider still attending our winter ball with the charming Miss Darrow. It would be a shame to return to Scotland without showing her London at its very best.

Kindest regards,

Gregory MacKinnon

Murdoch frowned as he reread the letter. It had not contained the information he expected. For the most part he did not wish to attend the expensive party the company was hosting in two days; on the other hand, now that Grey and MacKinnon had apologised it would be considered impolite to refuse their invitation.

It would be better to return to Darach on good terms with them, Murdoch realised. *For the sake of Sorcha, the security of the people who live on the Darrow land and the loch itself.*

He put down the letter to lie back beside her; Sorcha turned in her sleep to face him, blowing the same strand of hair away from her face over and over again until Murdoch relented and tucked it behind her ear. His fingertips grazed against her cheek, then traced the curve of her upper lip.

You would not have to worry about such human problems as greedy investors and rent payments if you accepted Lachlan's offer, Sorcha.

Immortality did not seem so odd to Murdoch. He had lived for over five hundred years, after all. A human's life was frightfully short and insignificant by comparison. It would be a joy for Sorcha to accept immortality and live forever alongside him.

Except for the fact that Sorcha did not want to live forever. She wished to remain as she was.

Murdoch's heart sank. If Sorcha stayed human then, sooner or later, she would be gone from his life. A decade would pass, then another and another, and she would grow old. Eventually she would die.

He could not bear it.

"I want to be with you my whole life," he murmured into Sorcha's ear, though she was too far wrapped up in her dreams to hear him. "I cannot imagine my world without you."

And then clarity struck like a bolt of lightning.

If Sorcha would not accept immortality, then Murdoch simply had to accept the opposite on her behalf.

It was a terrifying thought. Murdoch had struggled to be human over the past three weeks, but that was because he remained a kelpie on the inside, bound by laws of power and water and nature itself. If he could give all of that up then he could enjoy a mortal life just as easily as Sorcha did.

Can I really do this? Murdoch thought. *It will not be easy to become a human. Only the most powerful of faeries can grant such a wish. Which means...*

He made a face for nobody to see.

It meant asking Lachlan for a favour.

But all it took was one look at Sorcha's face – at the smallest of smiles that curled her lips as she slept – to tell Murdoch that he could do it. For all of her mortal flaws, from her impulsive, reckless nature to her stubborn insistence that she fix all her problems on her own, Sorcha was the one Murdoch loved. The one he dreamed of being with. He was determined to make that dream a reality.

If that meant getting down on his knees to beg the Seelie king for help then so be it.

CHAPTER TWENTY-FOUR

Lachlan

Ever since Lachlan had decided to call off the hunt for the white stag the animal had become something of a friend to him. Even now, in the bitter cold of mid-winter, the animal folded its legs beneath itself to sit beside Lachlan as he dozed beneath the empty boughs of an ancient oak tree. He loved oak more than any other kind of tree, for they reminded him of Sorcha; he had met her whilst standing upon the branches of one.

"I have not seen you in a while," he told the animal when it inched closer to him. Lachlan reached into his pocket and pulled out a handful of winter blackberries. The stag nosed at them curiously, eventually abandoning all caution and devouring them in one go. Lachlan smiled as the berries began to stain its muzzle a deep, dark purple, a colour akin to the blood of most water-dwelling monsters. He could almost imagine the stag possessing sharp, terrifying teeth within its jaws and using them to tear into the flesh of some unfortunate, supernatural creature.

Like a kelpie, Lachlan thought, his smile turning wicked as he imagined the beast's death.

But he could do nothing about the kelpie, nor the fact that Sorcha was alone with him down in London. *Not yet, at least. Tomorrow I will surprise Clara by whisking her off to the solstice revel.*

Lachlan couldn't wait.

The stag knocked its antlers against Lachlan's head, entangling several sharp points through his hair in the process. "Ow," he complained, carefully extricating his hair as the stag watched him with bright, almost amused eyes. *He is making fun of me,* Lachlan thought, *or he is trying to distract me.*

It took him nearly ten minutes to completely free his hair from the creature's antlers, after which he was left with a mess of knots around his head. On impulse Lachlan dug into the calf of his boot and pulled out a small dagger; the metal flashed in the pale winter sun and caused the stag to back away in fright.

"I guess you are wary of even your friends if they hold a blade," Lachlan murmured, before yanking a length of hair away from his head and cutting straight through it. He continued slicing away at his hair until the forest underbrush all around him was covered in it, glittering like threads of pure gold amongst moss and grass and acorns. By the time he was finished the stag had disappeared, only to be replaced by the almost ghostly figure of Ailith. The faerie was resplendent in a sheer, white gown that trailed behind her as she walked.

Ailith tutted in disapproval when she saw what Lachlan had done, then held out a hand for the dagger. "You were foolish to do this to yourself, Lachlan," she scolded, settling down behind him to fix what was presumably a mess of a hair cut. "You know I am much better than you at these things."

"And here you are, fixing it for me, so all is well that ends well."

"Are you nervous?"

Lachlan barked out a laugh. "Excuse me?"

"Are you nervous?" Ailith asked again, amusement plain as day in her voice as she methodically worked her way around Lachlan's hair with the dagger. "About heading down to London, I mean. One does not simply cut their hair on impulse like this unless they are trying to distract themselves."

He didn't reply. Of course Lachlan was nervous, for what if Sorcha declined his invitation to the solstice revel? She had no reason to, but even so...

I know she has feelings for the horse, he thought bitterly. *They were present two years ago, and they are still there now. There's a connection between the two of them that I do not understand.*

Lachlan wished he had met Sorcha even three days earlier than he had done. Just three days, with no interruption from the kelpie posing as Murdoch Buchanan, and perhaps Sorcha would have been his. *But then I would have ended up a fox, and she would have been stuck in the faerie realm at the mercy of my step family.*

"There, all done," Ailith said. She turned Lachlan around, working a spell upon the air in front of him until it hardened and turned into a mirror. "What do you think?"

Lachlan inspected his reflection with a critical eye. His hair was still long enough on top that it swept across his forehead and caught in his lashes, but the back and sides had been cropped into a layer of short, golden fuzz that felt pleasant against his skin when he ran his hands across it. Lachlan did not recall ever keeping his hair so short before.

He grinned. "I love it, Ailith. You have saved me."

"You will look particularly dashing for the revel, now," she said, stroking his hair away from his face as she did so. Her sapphire eyes were soft and lovely as she smiled. "Miss Sorcha will be so surprised. I'm sure you will have no problem bringing her back to the Seelie Court this time."

Lachlan chuckled. "I bloody well hope –"

"The Golden King."

Both Lachlan and Ailith turned to see who had spoken. A woman stood there, black hair long and thick and tangled down her back. She looked to be perhaps thirty, with a belly swollen with the final months of pregnancy. Her eyes were glassy; her expression manic. When Lachlan glanced at her feet he saw that she wore no shoes, and her feet were cut and bruised and blue from the cold. Clearly she had been walking for some time.

A human, he realised. *A human who has been enchanted. Who thought it clever to enchant a pregnant woman to walk through the woods in winter?*

"What is it, my fair lady?" he asked, taking off his thick, woollen cloak as he carefully approached the woman. He threw it over her shoulders, for she was shivering heavily, and motioned for her to sit down beneath the oak tree.

But the woman did not move. A wild smile that did

not meet her eyes stretched her mouth wide, and she recited: "*Never may my woes be relieved,*

Since pity is fled;

And tears and sighs and groans my weary days, my weary days

Of all joys have deprived."

A chill ran down Lachlan's spine. "Am I supposed to know what that means?" he pressed, frowning when he saw a flash of recognition cross Ailith's face.

"Miss Sorcha has sung this before," she said. "Once, when you were sleeping and the two of us could not, I shared a few cups of blackberry wine with her and she began to sing. It was unbearably sad. When I asked her who the song was for she said it was for the birds, but I did not think she was being truthful."

"A bird! A bird!" the woman called back, leaping from one foot to the other as if the ground beneath her toes was made of burning coals. "A singing bird in a silver cage. A silver cage to be locked forever and a day, if only she will sing."

"Sorcha," Lachlan whispered, not quite understanding the woman's riddles but knowing enough to be deathly afraid. He placed his hands on the woman's head, closed his eyes and said, "Sleep, and forget, and in the morning you will remember nothing of your enchantment or how you came to be here." The woman slumped against him, so Lachlan gently lowered her to the ground. He turned to Ailith. "Find her a bed to sleep in, and some clothes to wear, then work a location spell to find out where she came from."

"You wish to return her?" Ailith asked, a little unsure. "Surely it would be safer to have her live with us, Lachlan. She has clearly been enchanted for days!"

"She is pregnant!" Lachlan exclaimed, feeling sick that Ailith would even suggest keeping the woman in their realm, though it truly was the faerie way. "She must have a family! I will not break that family apart."

Lachlan knew it was Sorcha's doing that had him thinking this way; her love for her family was strong enough for her to have rebuffed his offer of immortality and a life in the Seelie Court time and time again. He no longer had the stomach to force anybody to leave the ones they adored unless it was their own choice.

Sorcha has affected my thinking more than I could have ever imagined. Two years ago I'd have never considered sending a human back from whence they came in a state of sanity.

Ailith nodded gravely. "You are heading down to London early, I am assuming?"

"Of course." He kissed her gently on her forehead. "I will change my clothes and be off. Look after our kingdom for me while I am gone."

"That is a given. Be careful, Lachlan."

"I shall be as careful as I can."

"That doesn't sound very careful at all."

Lachlan gave her a small smile. "Perhaps that is because I have never been careful. I will see you when I return."

And with that Lachlan fled back to the palace and to his chambers. He had no time to waste, but he knew he had to dress appropriately for the winter solstice revel. Something told Lachlan that his search for Sorcha would end up with him at it; after all, it was being hosted by the

163

Unseelie.

A singing bird in a silver cage, he thought. *Silver, like the Unseelie.*

Lachlan stared at his reflection, resplendent in all his green-and-gold finery, and hated himself. He might already be too late, and it was all his fault. "I should have stolen Sorcha away from London days and days ago," he snarled at his own face, then with a twirl of his pine-green cloak he was gone.

CHAPTER TWENTY-FIVE

Sorcha

The way Murdoch couldn't take his eyes off Sorcha caused a near-permanent blush across her cheeks. It had been that way for the last three days and now, dressed in a low-cut, feather-light, pale blue gown, his gaze was even more intense.

"Stop looking at me like that," Sorcha murmured, though she was smiling. She moved to tuck a lock of hair behind her ear but there was none; Mrs Ferguson had helped her pin her hair back with delicate silver chains and tiny, ornamental flowers.

"But you are so beautiful," Murdoch replied, squeezing Sorcha's hand with his own gloved one.

"So are you," Sorcha countered, which was the truth. He'd paired ebony, tight-fitting trousers with a high-collared white shirt and a silvery waistcoat intricately embroidered with a paisley pattern. Black, knee-high boots, a black velvet-lined tailcoat and a tall, round hat atop his curly hair completed the look.

"I had to look good enough to justify standing next to you," Murdoch said, only causing Sorcha's cheeks to flush ever more scarlet.

Their carriage was beginning to pull to a stop outside the location of the winter ball – a grand, stone-columned building that was lit up by lanterns atop ornate, iron poles. The lanterns reminded Sorcha of the Seelie revels she had attended in the past, though the flames in the faerie realm were all manner of colours rather than merely orange and yellow.

There were dozens of guests flooding into the hall when Murdoch and Sorcha finally stepped out of the carriage and onto the paved courtyard. He wrapped a royal blue, silken shawl around her shoulders before proffering his arm to her. She took it, smiling somewhat nervously up at him as they made their way into the building.

Murdoch noticed her discomfort. "What is wrong?" he asked, eyes widening when he spied the impressive, hulking evergreen trees that had been hauled in to line the walls all the way to the ballroom. A fiddle could be heard upon the air, as well as the sound of people's shoes dancing across the floor.

Sorcha's grip on his arm tightened. "I have not – this is the largest ball I have attended by far," she admitted. "There are so many people here. Are you sure it is a good idea to be here?"

"Oh, Sor – Miss Darrow," Murdoch said, only just remembering to correct himself now that they were in public, "I am sure we will have a grand time. And we have only to show our faces to Grey and MacKinnon to prove that we have made peace with them. Then we can leave, if that is what you truly wish. I simply do not want

166

to risk the safety of our home over something so inconsequential as manners."

"I suppose not."

"And besides," he added, gently encouraging Sorcha inside the ballroom with a hand on her back, "we never got to dance at the faerie revel two years ago, did we? Now is our chance to make up for that."

"You were pretending to be Lachlan and had just murdered his stepfather and stepbrother," Sorcha pointed out, wrinkling her nose at the memory. "Something tells me I would not have been in the mood for dancing even if I *hadn't* run off in horror."

Murdoch snickered, pulling away from Sorcha in order to remove his hat and place it on a table. "Granted, that probably wasn't the best way to put you in the mood for courtship," he murmured, turning to face Sorcha as a ten-piece orchestra began playing a new song, "so let me make it up to you now."

He bowed deeply, though there was a mischievous smile upon Murdoch's face that was anything but polite. He held out a hand. "May I have this dance, Miss Darrow?"

"I guess I can oblige your request, Mr Buchanan," Sorcha replied, curtsying before accepting Murdoch's hand.

Whoever thought I'd be dancing at a ball in London with the kelpie of Loch Lomond? she thought as they began to move through the steps of the dance. Sorcha was hesitant at first, for she was not so familiar with them, but it became quickly apparent that Murdoch Buchanan's memories granted the kelpie an adeptness with dancing that eventually put Sorcha at ease.

167

"You are much better at this than you are at walking, you know," she teased, laughing softly when a scandalised look crossed Murdoch's face.

"Humans are so slow on their two legs," he complained. "You are such frail, clumsy creatures."

"And yet here you are, dancing as one of them."

"And dressed as one of them."

"And talking like one of them."

"Having fallen for one of them."

Sorcha's heart twisted in her chest. She had thought things would get easier for her after they gave in to their desire for one another. Instead, when Murdoch gazed at her with unabashed, honest fondness Sorcha found that she could hardly stand it.

He will live forever and I will not, she thought, working hard to stop herself from crying. *It is the same problem as with Lachlan. Nothing will change that. If I want to live as a human then I will be gone before the kelpie can even blink.*

Murdoch's hand tightened on Sorcha's, and he pulled her a little closer to him. His expression had grown very, very serious, which Sorcha did not like one bit. "Miss Darrow," he began, "there is something I need to –"

"I – think I need some air," Sorcha interrupted, breaking away from Murdoch before he could finish his sentence. "I will not be long, I promise. I just –"

She rushed off, not really knowing what else she could say as an excuse. *What could I have told him?* Sorcha despaired, exiting the ballroom and turning down a random corridor between two evergreen trees without really looking where she was going. *That I care for him so deeply that I would do most anything for him? That I love him, but even that is not enough for me to be with him the way he wants me to? I saw the way he reacted to me declining Lachlan's offer of immortality. It shattered him.*

It was in that moment Sorcha realised just how much her refusal may well have shattered *Lachlan,* too. Since the faerie could not lie he had grown adept at concealing his emotions behind frivolity and pretty words, so much so that Sorcha had been able to pretend for the last two years that his desire to take Sorcha's mortality was still merely a whim. That his feelings for her would pass, and in no time at all he would forget about her.

In reality, Sorcha knew that had never been the case.

"I saw her go down there," a male voice Sorcha vaguely recognised muttered, causing her to hide behind a well-polished suit of armour to see who had spoken. A man with dark hair appeared at the entrance to the corridor, followed by an older man with equally dark hair.

That is Gregory MacKinnon and his son, Donald, Sorcha realised, inching further away from them as quietly as she was able.

The older man turned to the younger. "We will not get this opportunity again. Take her to the office whilst Buchanan is nowhere to be seen. Discreetly, Donald."

His son nodded before stalking down the corridor after Sorcha. She hardly dared to breathe as she flitted from shadow to shadow away from him, realising in the process that said shadows were twisting and warping and growing darker to help conceal her from the man. When Sorcha caught a glimmer in a mirror she realised what was happening.

The Unseelie, she thought, heart racing as Sorcha was forced to choose between which option posed a greater immediate risk to her. *If the Unseelie meant for me to die they would have killed me already, whereas I know these man cannot mean for anything good to happen to me,* she decided, glancing back over her shoulder at Donald MacKinnon as he continued purposefully towards her.

And then, just as Sorcha took another step down the corridor, a hand that had not been there before yanked her against the mirror, whilst another covered her mouth to stifle her cry of shock. Sorcha struggled for but a moment before growing rigid in sheer terror when she realised the hands were pulling her *through* the mirror, away from the hallway and the man who meant her harm.

"What is – let go of me!" Sorcha bit out the moment she had been completely pulled through the glassy surface, staring in shock as she watched Donald reach the very spot where she herself had only just been. It was like watching a moving painting; Sorcha reached out a hand to touch the mirror, only for it to be dragged away by the hand that had been on her mouth.

"I would not go back through there right now if I were you," a silky, familiar voice purred into her ear. "How about you attend a far more *exciting* party until you are no longer quite so hunted?"

Sorcha turned when the hands finally let her go. The silver-haired faerie who had inexorably been involved with her life from the moment she arrived in London stood there, no longer hiding under the glamour of a man.

His ears had grown long and pointed – longer than Lachlan's and the rest of the Seelie. His grey eyes had turned to liquid mercury, and his skin held a blue-silver tint Sorcha had only witnessed once before when she met Lachlan's stepbrother, Fergus.

He was dressed in midnight blue finery over a white, frothy shirt left unlaced to his navel; Sorcha's eyes trailed the deep V the material made of his skin before finding her way back to his face.

The faerie smiled a smile full of teeth filed to dangerously sharp points. "Won't you join our solstice revel, Miss Darrow, as the guest of the Unseelie king?"

Sorcha took a step back from him out of sheer disbelief. *Eirian. He is King Eirian.*

And though Sorcha wanted to say no – wished for nothing more than to crawl back through the mirror and scream for Murdoch to help her – as at the art exhibit when the faerie had asked her to walk around with him, Sorcha found she could do nothing but numbly accept the king's request.

CHAPTER TWENTY-SIX

Murdoch

Something is wrong.

Murdoch felt it in his very core, his mood flipping in an instant from deliriously happy to panic-stricken and painful.

Painful?

He clutched at his heart, bending double over his stomach. Murdoch's vision went hazy; he reached out a hand for the closest wall to stop himself from falling over.

"Sir?" a concerned gentleman said when he saw him. "Sir, are you quite all right?"

"Too much – too much brandy," Murdoch lied through gritted teeth. He could barely breathe. Barely talk. Barely stand.

Barely hold his shape.

Where is Sorcha?! Murdoch panicked, forcing himself back upright through sheer willpower alone. He stumbled around the ballroom, desperate to find her, but Sorcha was nowhere to be found. He exited down a long, gilded, empty corridor. "She can't have gone far," Murdoch panted, breaths coming shallow and ragged with every step he took. His lungs were closing in on him. "She can't have gone far, but somehow she is gone."

"How did you lose her, useless son of mine?" Murdoch heard a familiar voice mutter angrily from down a narrower, darker corridor to his left. Gregory MacKinnon stood there, fury contorting his features as he berated his son.

Don looked beyond perplexed. "Miss Darrow went down here alone, I swear it," he insisted. "It should have been simple to subdue her! But she...disappeared."

Disappeared? Disappeared where?

Then Murdoch noticed a large, silver-framed mirror hanging on the wall behind Don, and he realised with terrifying certainty what had happened to Sorcha.

No. Not the faerie realm. In travelling there – in being dragged there, Murdoch assumed – she had become separated from his bridle. But Sorcha was not *gone;* she was merely in a parallel, magically obscured world. Clearly the rules Lachlan had spelled onto Murdoch's bridle did not know how to deal with this, going by the pain he was in.

"You must *find her*," Gregory fumed, eyes wide as he pointed down the corridor. "Before Buchanan –"

"Before I what?"

Both MacKinnons flinched. Slowly they turned to face Murdoch, who staggered towards them with barely-contained contempt. He was shaking all over, and he knew he was going to lose his human form at any given moment, but right now he did not care. These men had been looking for Sorcha and he needed to know *why*.

"Mister Buchanan," Gregory said, voice altogether too panicked to match the smile he quickly plastered onto his face. He wiped at his brow. "We merely wished to speak to Miss Darrow ourselves, to see if – to see if she might be convinced to sell her land to us after all. We had never posed the question to her directly before."

"I do not believe you," Murdoch spat, stalking forward another step or two. He resisted the urge to use the wall for support. "I heard you talk about *subduing* her. What were you planning to do to Miss Darrow?"

"N-nothing," Don stuttered, terrified. It was the terror on his face that told Murdoch he was already changing form, for the man was of a similar height and build to Mr Buchanan. If it came down to a fight the father and son in front of him may well have overpowered Murdoch.

If he were human.

"*What were you planning to do to Miss Darrow?*" Murdoch demanded once more, catching his gloved hands shimmering and shaking out of the corner of his eye. And then, between one moment and the next, Murdoch's line of sight grew much taller, and the corridor seemed altogether much smaller. Don swallowed back a cry; his father stumbled away from the monster that had appeared before him.

"What are you?" Gregory whispered, eyes so wide that Murdoch could see white all around his irises.

Murdoch's hooves scratched and screeched across

174

the floor as he dragged himself closer to the two men. *Something still isn't right,* he realised, for the lurching, twisting feeling in his stomach had not disappeared. But he could deal with that later; first he had to sort out Gregory and Donald MacKinnon.

When he bared his teeth and let out a low snarl the younger man slipped and fell to the floor, scrambling backwards until he reached his father. He fumbled through his pocket and brought out a bible, holding it out in front of him with a wildly trembling hand.

Murdoch merely laughed. "You think I am unholy? Your petty religion can do nothing to me. Where is Miss Darrow?"

"We do not know!" Gregory said, letting out a garbled cry when Murdoch reared onto his hind legs and crashed back down inches from his face. "I swear we don't!"

"I was following her but she disappeared!" Don chimed in, eyes never leaving Murdoch's mouthful of sickeningly sharp teeth. "All we were going to do was force her to sign over the Darrow land, I swear!"

"*Force her?*" Murdoch snarled. "You were going to force my bride to do something she expressly did not wish to do, and all behind my back? Was this the real reason you wanted us to attend the ball tonight even after what was said at your home?"

The silence from Gregory MacKinnon was deafening. Murdoch could not stand to look at him; he ground his hooves into the marble floor until it cracked beneath the man's feet. Gregory tried to back further away, but there was no more corridor left for him to do so.

He stared up at Murdoch's wild, inhuman face. "We did not know - how were we to know that you were not - not -"

"Human? It should not have mattered!" he screamed, incandescent with rage. "But now you will pay. One does not cross a kelpie and live to tell the tale."

"Please!" Don begged, kicking away from Murdoch as if he might somehow avoid him by escaping along the left side of the corridor; Murdoch swatted him against the wall as if he weighed nothing at all. A sickening crack filled the air as the man hit his head then slumped, motionless, to the floor.

Gregory stared at the slack body of his son with stark-white horror. Blood was beginning to pool beneath Don's head, filling Murdoch's nose with the intoxicating scent of death and destruction. His nostrils flared, and he bent low to pin Gregory MacKinnon beneath his hooves.

"D-do not kill me!" he begged. "We will leave your home well enough alone, I assure you! If you kill me then my colleagues will not know to abandon the project!"

"I should kill you *all*."

"They did not know my son and I were planning to do this," Gregory insisted. "Please, Mr Buchanan -"

"*That is not who I am.*"

But even as Murdoch spoke he felt his form beginning to revert back to the man in question. He let out an involuntary cry, knocked Gregory unconscious, then shuffled backwards out of the corridor until he had enough space to turn himself around. His hooves clacked against marble and tile and stone as he galloped through the hall, frantic to find an exit even as people screeched at the sight of him and desperately dodged out of the way.

By the time Murdoch reached the cold release of bitter winter air he had turned back into a man again, but not for long. For no sooner than he reached the line of carriages waiting to take party-goers home he transformed once more, so with a roar he turned in the direction of the nearest body of water and plunged straight into it.

Lachlan, Murdoch thought, almost blind with pain. *I must get to Lachlan. Only he can help me now.*

Murdoch had no idea how he was supposed to get all the way back to Loch Lomond when he kept changing form every five minutes, but he had to try. Sorcha's life depended on it. He only hoped he would not reach Lachlan too late to help her.

And so it was to Murdoch's great surprise and fortune when, barely out of London, he crashed straight into the Seelie king himself between jumps from one body of water to the next. The faerie's eyes widened in baffled disbelief as he watched Murdoch change from kelpie to man right in front of him, then back again and again and again, so uncontrollably fast that Murdoch could no longer see or breathe as he collapsed to the ground at Lachlan's feet.

If this kept on going for much longer Murdoch knew that he would die.

"Is that – what is going on with you?!" Lachlan demanded, though Murdoch could scarcely hear him. "Why do you keep changing? Where is Sorcha?" He crunched a foot against Murdoch's shoulder when he did not answer. "*Where is Sorcha?*" he asked again, fear colouring his tone this time instead of anger.

It took everything Murdoch had to find the strength to reply.

"Gone."

CHAPTER TWENTY-SEVEN

Lachlan

Lachlan had been slipping in and out of the faerie realm to travel to London as fast as possible, for given the infuriating riddle he'd been threatened with he knew he did not have much time to reach Sorcha.

So what was the kelpie of Loch Lomond doing out here, all alone, shape-shifting so quickly that it hurt Lachlan's eyes to watch him change form? He was supposed to be protecting Sorcha. But if she was nowhere to be seen, and Murdoch could not hold his shape, then –

"The Unseelie have taken her, haven't they?" Lachlan demanded, blood turning to ice as he slammed his foot against the kelpie's shoulder. He was a man now, but the bubbling of his skin told Lachlan that he would change again at any given moment. "How in the name of the bloody forest did you allow them to *take her*?!"

"Mirror," Murdoch gasped. The whites of his eyes

were red; dark, evil-looking blood was beginning to leak from them to stain his face. "A mirror. They took her through a..." But then the kelpie began to scream, and he reverted to his original form once more.

Lachlan couldn't stand the noise. He kicked at the beast, furious that he could not simply let Murdoch die. So many of his problems would be solved if he were gone, after all, but now he needed his help. Lachlan could not storm the Unseelie Court without back-up.

"Damn you to death, horse!" he screeched in response to the kelpie's cries, bending low to place his hands over the bridle that was currently the source of all the monster's pain. Forcing himself to concentrate through all his fear and panic and anger, Lachlan closed his eyes and slowly but surely unravelled the binding magic he had placed upon the item.

When he stood back up and opened his eyes the kelpie had returned to the form of Murdoch Buchanan once more, his bridle an innocuous silver chain hanging around his neck, barely visible over the high collar of his shirt. The man who was not a man retched and heaved upon the grass, tremors wracking through his body so violently that Lachlan thought Murdoch was in danger of breaking every bone in his body.

"Get yourself together," he spat. "We have no time to waste. How long has Sorcha been missing?"

Murdoch glared up at him, taking a deep, shuddering breath before forcing himself onto unsteady feet. Lachlan realised he was dressed up as if he had been at a formal dance, though he was drenched from head to toe.

"T-twenty minutes," Murdoch finally bit out. He wiped the back of a hand across his forehead, then smeared away the blood that had trickled down his cheeks. "Mister Buchanan's colleagues were attempting to corner her on her own, but she disappeared through a mirror."

"But why was she *alone*? I warned her not to be!"

Murdoch flinched at this, but then he scowled. "She was gone from my side for but five minutes, faerie. If that damn MacKinnon hadn't stalked her down a corridor then –"

"And that is your fault!" Lachlan countered. "I should never have allowed Sorcha to come down here with you. Every second since the two of you left I have regretted it."

"You could not have forbidden her from going. She would have gone anyway."

"Do you think I do not *know* that?" Lachlan stormed off for a few seconds, thinking that perhaps it was not worth saving the kelpie's life after all, but then he stopped. He pinched the bridge of his nose, a low growl forming in his throat that he struggled not to let loose. *I should have locked Sorcha up. I should have found out her full name and enchanted her to stay with me. She might have hated me but she would have been safe. And now the Unseelie have her.*

With a long, frustrated sigh, Lachlan muttered, "How does she do it?"

A pause. "Do what, exactly?"

"Get herself embroiled in inhuman schemes without having a single clue about them, of course!" Lachlan yelled, losing his temper once more. He looked at the kelpie over his shoulder, unabashedly baring his teeth in the process. "She knew nothing of the Unseelie and yet they followed her through the streets of London, taunting her."

"And snuck into my house through the mirrors to leave her a warning."

Lachlan stilled. He had not known about that. "... what did the warning say?" he asked, very, very quietly.

"*To the kelpie's bride*," Murdoch recited, shaking himself of water in the process like a dog, "*we suggest you choose your company a little more wisely in the days to come.* I assumed they were warning her against interacting with me, since I murdered Innis and Fergus."

"As if I needed to be reminded of that," Lachlan growled. But then he considered the Unseelie threat without the cloud of resentment he held towards the kelpie hanging over him, and he frowned. "It may not be about you. It could be about me."

The troubled look on Murdoch's face confirmed Lachlan's suspicions. "Sorcha believed that might be the case, I think. She was concerned it was about us both."

They exchanged a wary, meaningful glance. They both knew what that meant: they could be walking right into a trap by going after Sorcha.

Knowing that changed nothing at all.

With an overwhelming sense of foreboding, Lachlan waved a hand in Murdoch's direction and watched as the man's clothes and hair and skin dried and tidied themselves in an instant.

"Why did you do that?" Murdoch demanded, closing the gap between them with a scandalised look on his face. "I do not need your -"

"You will stand out if you show up to the Unseelie

solstice revel looking like a drowned man," Lachlan cut in. He sidled a glance at the kelpie out of the corner of his eye. "Even though that is what you are."

"Charming."

"Have you stopped dying yet?"

"...almost."

"Then come," Lachlan said, walking towards a nearby grove of pine trees with both his hands held out in front of him. "We have a revel to interrupt, and a damsel to rescue."

"Do not let Sorcha hear you call her that."

Lachlan grinned a vicious grin. "No; I suppose you are right. But she is a damsel in need of rescue nonetheless, and we have a silver dragon going by the name of Eirian to slay."

CHAPTER TWENTY-EIGHT

Sorcha

There was absolutely no doubt that the revel King Eirian led Sorcha to was the work of the fae, though everything about the celebration seemed altogether darker and more sinister than those hosted by the Seelie Court.

It wasn't held outside, for a start. The massive, high-ceilinged hall Eirian pulled Sorcha into was opulent and glittering but it was clear that it was very, very old. Ancient, even. Chandeliers of burnished silver hung from the ceiling, and candlesticks of a similar metal sat atop long, gnarled tables overladen with food so colourful and exotic Sorcha thought for a moment that it could not possibly be real. Wax from the candles steadily melted down onto the tables as slow, molten rivers before solidifying into large clumps the colour of snow.

Thick, velvet curtains of deepest purple and midnight blue adorned the walls, draping down onto the floor where groups of fae lay upon the fabric and lost themselves in each other. In the corners of the hall were far more translucent, silvery curtains, gently billowing and floating all around as if caught upon the wind.

The light in the room seemed to flicker and change with every blink Sorcha took, imitating the glimmers she had noticed reflected at her back in the human world. There were dozens of mirrors around her now, too, haphazardly lining the walls in all shapes and sizes and manner of frames. Wooden. Gilded. New. Crumbling with age. Scorched and melted. Shining and perfect.

On a plinth in the centre of the room a string quartet was playing a haunting, almost familiar melody, but when Sorcha tried to place it she found that it was impossible.

A song from a dream, perhaps, she thought, moving through a crowd of intoxicated, masked creatures who eagerly parted for their king. Sorcha was barely aware of the fact she was following him, so entranced by the scene around her as she was.

That was when she began to notice individual revellers. A burly faerie in the corner with a river nymph on either of his arms, polishing his horns with what could have been wine but was probably blood. A cat-like, winged creature stalking across a trestle table to steal a plate of golden apples. A group of seven impossibly beautiful, blue-skinned faeries lying in a pit of pillows, limbs twisted and entwined together as their faces contorted in pleasure.

Sorcha's cheeks grew red, and she looked away, but then all the blood quickly drained from her face when she focused her gaze on the musicians. They were human, which was not so uncommon at a faerie revel, and they were enchanted, which was even less of a rarity, but it was the condition of them that made Sorcha's stomach turn.

Their fingers were raw and bloody, some of them worked down to the bone, and yet still they continued to play their instruments with mad smiles on their faces and not an ounce of pain in their eyes.

Sorcha caught sight of more humans in the crowd after that; she wished she hadn't. Most all of them were suffering in one way or another, though they were blissfully unaware of their agony. Two mortal men were fighting to the death, one of them bleeding heavily from an ugly gash in his leg even as he tore into his opponent's arm with his teeth. A group of Unseelie surrounded them, cheering and drinking and gambling on who would win.

And there was a small child in a corner crying for his mother, who had been forced to drink faerie wine and was now pleasuring a twisted creature twice her size.

When Sorcha witnessed a girl younger than herself being eaten alive, laughing delightedly even as a faerie with the scales of a snake gorged on her innards, she froze to the spot out of fear she would collapse and never get back up.

Eirian turned to face her when he realised Sorcha had ceased walking. His eyes followed her line of sight, a sigh passing his lips when he realised what had caused such an ashen expression to spread across her face. "We are the Unseelie, lass," he said, taking Sorcha's hand in his own and pulling her towards a table laden with glasses of strange-coloured liquids. "I would have assumed that, given your familiarity with our brethren, you would be aware of our natures."

Sorcha stared at him in horror, then gulped down

her fear and tried her best to put herself back together. She had walked into the proverbial lion's den, except the lion had been replaced with creatures far more dark and dangerous. If she was not careful then she would become their prey before the moon truly rose into the sky that night.

"I am afraid I do not have the *stomach* for such entertainment," she told Eirian, "though I imagine you knew that already."

The grin he gave her was predatory. "I did surmise as much," he said, "though I will eagerly admit to taking much pleasure out of watching you react to said entertainments. Have a drink, Miss Darrow. Our blackberry wine rivals anything the Seelie Court makes."

But Sorcha knew better than to accept the glass of black wine Eirian offered her. Lachlan and Ailith ensured that she never consumed anything made of faerie flora and fauna, for if she did then not only would Sorcha have fallen into a giddy, prone-to-hallucinations state for hours on end, but she would no longer have been able to leave the faerie realm of her own free will.

"Thank you for the offer, King Eirian," Sorcha said, pushing away the glass, "but I must refuse."

"You are clever."

"I am experienced more than I am clever," she replied, glancing around the revel as she did so. The bloody-fingered musicians kept drawing her eye again and again. "You did not think to entrap me here like the other poor mortals attending your festivities, did you?"

"If I did not try then I could not call myself a faerie," Eirian laughed. He swept Sorcha away from the table and towards a group of dancing faeries. Their energy was frenetic, as if they might never stop dancing even if it killed them. Sorcha knew that, for humans, it often did. "But I do have more important motives for inviting you here than to trick you."

Sorcha frowned. "I do not believe that."

"Yet I cannot lie," he countered. His eyes slid across Sorcha's dress in a way that made her wildly uncomfortable, but when she tried to look away Eirian grabbed her chin with a long-fingered hand and held it in place. "You are a bonnie girl, as your folk would say," he began, calculating eyes locked on hers, "but I believe you can be more beautiful still. That dress of yours is too...human. Allow me to rectify that."

"I do not –" Sorcha bit out, but her words caught in her throat as she was enveloped in a wave of magic. The sleeves of her gown disappeared, and the material became diaphanous, trailing behind her in soft waves of silvery, iridescent fabric. The neckline grew lower, too, almost as low as the Unseelie king's shirt, revealing far more of the curves of her breasts than Sorcha was used to.

Sorcha reached a hand up to her hair as it came almost entirely undone, tumbling around her shoulders and down her back in wild, sensuous curls. Her ears felt heavy, and when Sorcha caught her reflection in a mirror she saw that many silver crescent moons now hung from them on impossibly delicate chains. A similarly-designed circlet kept her hair away from her face, and lashings of silver lined her eyes.

All around Sorcha faeries paused from their activities to stare at her with ravenous, unbridled desire. *If I can feel their king's magic working upon me then it must be overpowering to them,* she thought, looking back at

Eirian to see a smug expression upon his face.

"Much better," he murmured. Without turning from her, he waved a hand towards the musicians and the melody changed to something Sorcha most definitely recognised.

I sang this through the streets of London when I was being stalked.

"Won't you sing for me?" Eirian asked, voice like honey as he pulled Sorcha further into the crowd of dancers. She swatted away their greedy hands as they pawed at her and begged her to say yes.

"I will not," Sorcha replied, fighting hard to keep her voice firm and steady. After Lachlan's warning not to give the Unseelie anything she was determined to refuse any and all of their requests, no matter how innocuous they seemed to be.

Eirian looked as if his heart had been broken. "Then won't you dance?" he asked instead, holding out a hand for Sorcha to take.

"If I dance I will not be able to stop," she said, just barely moving out of the way as a faerie covered in wicked-looking spines twirled past her.

But the Unseelie king took her hand regardless. "If I promise you that you can stop at any time, will you agree to dance?"

"I –"

Sorcha frowned. If she was allowed to stop when she wished to then in theory dancing would do no harm to her at all. And it would give her time to work out what to do next, and serve as a distraction from the horrors all around her.

Do not do it, the sensible part of her brain screamed, but Sorcha nodded her head at Eirian regardless.

"Then I shall dance," Sorcha said, and so she did.

CHAPTER TWENTY-NINE

Murdoch

Just a flicker. Just a glimpse. That was all Murdoch needed to make out Sorcha through the throng of Unseelie revellers, so why could he not find her?

"Fox, we should split up until one of us finds her," he told Lachlan, who winced at the insult but nodded regardless.

"If you find her first I shall cause a commotion to allow you to get her out of here," Lachlan said, a determined glint in his golden eyes as he scanned the crowd. "I expect you to do the same."

"Of course. May the best man find her first."

Under ordinary circumstances both of them may have laughed bitterly at the ironic comment, but there was absolutely nothing ordinary about a kelpie and a faerie king searching for a mortal at an Unseelie revel.

Lachlan stalked away without another word, leaving Murdoch to prowl around the very edges of the hall to take in his surroundings, ignoring the glazed-over eyes of the unfortunate mortals who had found themselves part of the menu for tonight's revel.

He had been to one other such celebration four hundred years earlier, though entirely by accident. A witch who had done him wrong fled to the Unseelie realm, attempting to hide herself in the throng of hedonistic faeries as they danced the solstice away. What she had not anticipated was just how hungry for violence the Unseelie were, and how eagerly they gave her up in order to witness Murdoch tear her apart limb from limb.

That was the first time Murdoch had willingly done something that a faerie wanted him to do, because it aligned with his own interests.

Working with Lachlan to save Sorcha was the second.

Murdoch spent almost twenty minutes skirting the edges of the revel, growing ever more frustrated that he could not spot Sorcha. Faerie folk were beginning to take notice of him, the lower kinds grinning at him as if they believed him to be mortal prey whilst the more magically-inclined onces inched back when he grew near, intimidated by the sheer power the kelpie possessed.

Good, Murdoch thought as he finally carved a path through the crowd. *Leave me be. Let me find her. Let me see –*

He froze.

For there was Sorcha, dressed all in glittering, flowing silver like an ethereal winter queen. Murdoch's heart throbbed painfully in his chest at the mere sight of her. He was beyond relieved when he noticed her eyes were not glazed over, nor was there a vague smile upon her face. *She is not enchanted,* he sighed. *That is one point in our favour.*

But Sorcha had not noticed Murdoch's presence, too absorbed in the attentions of the silver-haired faerie who was leading her through a dance. He seemed eerily familiar to Murdoch, though he did not know why. And then it hit him: the faerie was the one responsible for cornering Sorcha at the art exhibit. He had been cloaked in a glamour before, but Murdoch could see it clearly now that he was looking at the Unseelie in question.

But that...that can't be right, Murdoch thought, growing increasingly frantic as he pushed through the crowd to reach Sorcha. But the creatures all around him pushed back, keeping Murdoch constantly out of reach and sight of her. *That can't be the faerie who was after her.*

If Murdoch hadn't known any better, he could have sworn the one Sorcha was dancing with was the Unseelie king himself.

Lachlan

"The Seelie king! The Seelie king is here!" a shimmering, naked faerie announced excitedly upon spotting Lachlan – a member of his own race, ventured down to the Unseelie realm alongside a group of other like-minded fae for a night of riotous, violent fun.

He forced a smile on his face. "Of course I am here," Lachlan said. "How would it look if I did not show up to celebrate with my brethren?"

Lachlan did not wait for an answer, instead winding his way through the revel as quickly as he could. But he was stopped at almost every opportunity, claws and nails and fingertips alike dragging at his sleeves to pull him into some game or dance or gamble. When someone forced a goblet of amber whisky into his hand Lachlan poured it down his throat simply to appease them, though under any other circumstance he would have savoured every last drop of the stuff.

"Where are you, Clara?" he muttered, reverting to her false name in case anybody was listening. The last thing he needed was for hundreds of sharp-toothed, bloodthirsty Unseelie to learn even one third of her true name. "Just where are you?"

And then as if on command he saw her, more enchantingly beautiful than Lachlan had ever seen her before. *More beautiful than Ailith, even,* he thought, stopping in his tracks to stare unabashedly at the mortal woman who had stolen his heart. The cut of Sorcha's dress was so daring that one wrong move would have revealed every inch of her skin, but the translucent material somehow stayed perfectly in place as she danced.

Danced.

Lachlan bit back a scream.

Sorcha was dancing with King Eirian.

"Clara!" he called, but then Lachlan was swept away by the crowd, and she disappeared from his sight.

Sorcha

Was that...Murdoch? And – Lachlan? Sorcha thought. *But it couldn't be. Murdoch is back at the winter ball, and that golden faerie does not possess Lachlan's long hair.*

"Something the matter?"

194

She frowned at King Eirian, who pulled her a little closer in response. "I think I – may have seen someone I know," she said, "but I must have been wrong." *Although Lachlan could well be here. He is the Seelie king; perhaps I am not imagining him.*

Eirian twirled Sorcha under his arm, laughing all the while. "They got here faster than I expected."

"You were...I was not imagining the kelpie and Lachlan?"

"I would not think so given that you are here, Miss Darrow," the faerie said, keeping his tone conversational even as his silver eyes grew sharper and his grin more vicious.

Sorcha began searching desperately for another glimpse of golden skin or Murdoch's dark, curly hair as Eirian spun her around and around in time with the dancers. She was growing dizzy, and her feet were beginning to hurt. "I think I would like to stop and find them," she told him, the words coming out a little breathless.

But Eirian merely laughed again. "Do you know how much effort was put into ensuring that you and your dear kelpie came down to London, Miss Darrow?" he asked, sliding a hand down to the small of Sorcha's back to prevent her from pulling away. He cocked his head to the side, watching her face as a hawk might watch a rabbit. "So much magic was put into manipulating those men who worked with Mr Buchanan into pushing on with procuring the Darrow land, and even more into watching your every move."

A shiver ran up Sorcha's spine from where Eirian's fingertips touched it. "You have been...you planned everything from the very start?"

"Why of course," he said simply. "I could not risk my crown on mere *chance,* could I? Not after what happened last time."

"Last time?" Sorcha parroted back, but then she shook her head in an attempt to clear it. "I wish to stop dancing. You said I could stop dancing whenever I wanted to."

But King Eirian bent his head and chuckled softly against her ear. "I said you could stop, Miss Darrow, but not that anybody else would *let* you. Have fun at the revel."

"I – no, I don't want this!" Sorcha cried, as he handed her off to the faerie with blood-soaked horns she had spotted earlier. The Unseelie king merely threw back his head and laughed, accepting the hand of another partner as Sorcha was spun further and further away from him. She pushed against the burly creature who was now forcing her to dance, but his arms were thick with muscle and refused to let her go.

"You are his now, girlie," the faerie grinned, displaying a mouth full of vicious teeth even redder than his horns. "There is no point in struggling."

And yet struggle was what Sorcha tried and tried and tried to do, fighting against every new faerie she was thrown into the arms of. Her muscles ached, and her feet felt raw and slashed to ribbons, but still Sorcha was forced to dance despite her protests. All around her the Unseelie were laughing at her, but none so loudly as their king.

His voice was in her head, taunting her. Threatening her.

"Let. Her. Go."

196

This new voice was cold and demanding and familiar, cutting through the noise of the revel like a knife made of ice. All at once the laughter around Sorcha came to stop. Something was awry; there was a darkness upon the air that not a single creature seemed to like. Slowly – very slowly – individual faeries began to stop dancing and fighting and kissing each other. Sorcha recognised the looks upon their faces. They were dying.

Drowning.

The kelpie, Sorcha thought, more relieved than she thought she'd ever be at the sight of burgeoning mass murder. She pulled away from the arms of the faerie who had been dancing with her, for they had stopped in horror, but then Eirian reappeared in front of Sorcha and dragged her into his embrace.

"He cannot help you," the Unseelie king said, a delighted, wicked smile upon his face as he continued the dance. "Nobody can. So won't you sing for me, Miss Darrow?"

A feeling of dread spread through her as Sorcha realised she was getting closer and closer to saying *yes.*

CHAPTER THIRTY

Murdoch

With every faerie laid to waste upon the ground Murdoch's soul filled with dark, vicious, unrelenting pleasure. Back when he had attacked the Seelie Court he'd drowned everyone using the burn that ran around the revel grounds, but here the kelpie had no such external sources of water to utilise.

But he was livid. Murderous. More focused than he had ever been in his entire life.

And so it was that filling the lungs of the Unseelie with their own blood was barely a challenge for Murdoch, though his range was limited to perhaps ten or so creatures at a time. He stalked through the crowd, targeting the monsters who were torturing children and raping mortal women first, and when he caught Lachlan's eye the golden faerie did not stop him.

Rather, the Seelie king acted like a mortal himself and began punching faeries in the face, not stopping until they were bloody and unconscious.

If he uses his magic against them then it could be considered an act of war, Murdoch realised. *Until he knows Eirian's intentions for sure he cannot use his full powers.*

"Useless fox!" Murdoch roared, bodily picking up a naked, blue-skinned Unseelie and flinging her out of his path. He could see Sorcha once more in the arms of King Eirian, her face wet with tears as she cried and begged to be let go.

Her misery only fuelled Murdoch's power.

"Get me to Eirian and you will see how useless I am!" Lachlan growled at Murdoch when they found themselves fighting beside each other. "Just keep slaughtering his people. You're good at that."

"I never expected a compliment from you."

"And I never thought you'd willingly fight alongside me, but there's a first time for everything."

All around them more and more revellers were stopping what they were doing, climbing over each other in their haste to get as far away from Murdoch as possible. But the dancers were still dancing and the musicians were still playing, for King Eirian was spinning Sorcha around and around and they were all eager to please him.

When the two of them passed a table Eirian picked up a glass of vibrant, luminous green liquid and held it up to Sorcha's lips. "Drink from this and all your pain will go away," Murdoch heard the king tell her, his voice so soft and seductive that Murdoch knew Sorcha would only be able to resist his charms for so long.

"Kelpie, her feet," Lachlan growled, kicking a goat-eyed faerie to the ground when it tried to attack

Murdoch. So he turned his gaze to Sorcha's feet, and his eyes grew glassy.

Gone were her slippers, leaving Sorcha's feet bare to everything on the floor. They were torn to shreds; bloody, bruised and blackened, leaving a trail of crimson wherever she danced. She could barely stand, but still Eirian was making her dance. Sorcha's face was contorted in pain, trying in vain to avoid the goblet of faerie wine the Unseelie king held to her lips as he urged her to drink.

She was going to take it. Murdoch knew she was going to take it.

He dropped his human form and charged forward, crushing every unfortunate creature that found its way in front of him beneath his hooves. Murdoch screamed, slashing through bone and sinew with his razor-sharp teeth whenever he grabbed hold of a faerie.

"Let her go!" he demanded, in a voice so loud the silvered chandeliers above his head trembled and the clamour all around him seemed like nothing but whispers.

"Kindly stop murdering my people and I shall consider it," King Eirian said, infuriatingly calm, when Murdoch was but seconds away from him. He tried to move closer to the faerie – to steal Sorcha right out of his grasp – but something kept pushing Murdoch's entire body away whenever he got within ten feet of the king.

"Do it," Lachlan told Murdoch, taking a step through whatever barrier was stopping Murdoch from moving forward as if there was nothing there at all. The faerie gave him a side-long glance. "We may still need your strength, so preserve it. But for now it's my turn, horse."

Murdoch was loathe to listen to him. He wanted to continue thrashing his way through the revel, destroying everything and everyone he came across until Sorcha was his again, but with a deep, trembling breath the kelpie struggled back to his human form.

Sorcha's eyes darted from Murdoch's face to Lachlan's and then back once more to Murdoch's. "I am s-sorry," she sobbed, barely audible over the noise all around her but cutting straight through to Murdoch nonetheless. "I'm sorry I –"

"You do not need to apologise to *them,* Miss Darrow," Eirian crooned, stroking a finger down her face even as he kept the faerie wine dangerously close to her mouth. "It is their fault that you are in this position in the first place."

Murdoch scowled at the comment, though its truthfulness was like an arrow to his heart. "You said you would let her go if I stopped!" he cried.

"No, he said he would consider it," Lachlan said, throwing a warning glare at Murdoch when he tried to move forward and met Eirian's invisible barrier once more.

The Unseelie king chuckled softly. "That is correct, my dear Lachlan," he murmured, "but I would rather not have the kelpie begin another rampage." Murdoch dared not breathe when Eirian shifted the goblet in front of Sorcha's face, but then he pulled it away from her and poured the venomously green wine onto the floor, soaking the stone beneath his feet a dark and dangerous colour.

"Give her back," Murdoch demanded between ragged breaths. "The fox and I are here, which was clearly your intention, so let the mortal go."

"Oh, I think not."

Lachlan exchanged an uncertain glance with Murdoch. There was a frown creasing his brow, telling the kelpie that he was currently thinking very hard of how to get Sorcha out of her captivity without accidentally agreeing to anything King Eirian said.

But Murdoch did not care about being cautious. If it meant saving Sorcha, he would agree to anything.

"What is that you want, then?" he asked, moving out of the way when Lachlan made to punch his face in frustration. "To let Miss Darrow go, what is it that you want?"

The grin that spread across Eirian's face was far more wicked than any Lachlan or Murdoch himself could ever have been capable of.

"Why, I want your lives, of course."

CHAPTER THIRTY-ONE

Sorcha

"No!" Sorcha cried out, the moment the Unseelie king voiced his demand. She pulled on his sleeve, emboldened by her fear. "You cannot kill them! What have they done to deserve that?"

When Eirian snaked an arm around her waist and kissed her forehead Sorcha recoiled, and Lachlan yowled in outrage. "Why, the two of them together murdered my beloved brother, Innis, and my dear little nephew, Fergus," he explained, as if it was obvious. "It is only natural that I have the heads of those that slew them with cold, black iron."

Sorcha froze. She stared at the tense, furious figures of Lachlan and Murdoch as they realised they were fully caught in Eirian's trap. Lachlan took a step forward, for whatever magic the Unseelie king had cast around himself and Sorcha clearly had no effect on him. Murdoch seemed to grow even angrier that he could not break through.

"The kelpie murdered your family," Lachlan said, choosing his words very, very carefully. "You can kill him for his crimes if you have the power to do so."

"Lachlan, you cannot mean –"

"Do not interfere, Clara!" the golden faerie warned. "He is guilty and he knows it – *you* know it!"

"It is all right, Miss Darrow," Murdoch reassured, giving Sorcha a small, reassuring smile before turning his gaze to Eirian. "The one who murdered your Unseelie kin was indeed me, as the fox said."

"And yet you let it happen," King Eirian pointed out, waving lazily at Lachlan as he spoke.

Lachlan bristled. "They had cursed me, as well you know!"

"A matter to be resolved between our two families, *not* at the hands of a kelpie."

"I was hardly in a position to stop him," Lachlan insisted. "Nobody could stop him."

"Nobody?"

Sorcha felt Eirian's hand twitch against her waist, and she realised Lachlan had slipped up. *He just told the Unseelie king that nobody in his Court was strong enough to destroy the kelpie. Now Eirian knows the full extent – or limit – of their power.*

Going by the grin on Eirian's face, he was delighted by this piece of information.

Lachlan looked just about ready to hang himself. It was not like him to slip up in such a manner, which meant he must have been truly rattled. *It is my fault,* Sorcha thought, wincing as she shifted slightly on her bleeding feet. *I was lured here to be used as a bargaining chip, and it is working.*

"You underestimate how strong I am, Unseelie," Murdoch thundered, drawing all of their attention back to him. Several nearby faeries stumbled away, hands scrabbling at their throats as they retched and choked on seemingly nothing at all. When the feeling finally abated they fled the revel, followed by a multitude of other creatures who had not yet left out of sheer interest for the confrontation that had interrupted their celebrations.

Eirian cocked his head to one side. "Perhaps. You are indeed formidable; there is no significant body of water in sight and yet you can kill with ease. It is impressive how strong you are."

Sorcha did not know if that meant the Unseelie king was also too weak to destroy Murdoch, or if he could handle the kelpie with ease despite the creature's strength.

She did not wish to find out.

Behind them the poor, doomed, mortal musicians began to play an unsettling melody that caused Sorcha's heart to beat erratically. She wanted to bolt from Eirian's side – was desperate to – but a subtle slide of his hand against her hip warned Sorcha that she would not get very far if she tried, especially on her injured feet.

"I will not let you kill me for something I did not do and could not prevent," Lachlan said after a tense moment of silence. "And I have not used my powers as the Seelie king against your kind. You have no recourse to demand anything from me."

Eirian shrugged emphatically. "And yet here I am, demanding your life nonetheless. But I am not a heartless king," he said, a hideous smile upon his face, "and I am open to bargains of equal value."

Lachlan and Murdoch stared at each other, then in unison looked at Sorcha just as Eirian turned her head to look at *him*.

"This mortal is dear to you," he sneered. "So dear, in fact, that you have risked everything to come here and save her. For the sake of the Seelie, Lachlan, you should not have come to her aid. And you, kelpie," he glanced at Murdoch before returning his mercurial eyes to Sorcha's, "if you did not wish to be controlled or destroyed you should have abandoned her, too. But you did not. I admit that I am curious as to why..."

When Eirian raised a finger to Sorcha's lips she bit it, gnashing her teeth into his flesh in her desperation to break through to the bone. But she barely left a scratch, and when Eirian pulled his hand away he laughed as if Sorcha had just done something incredibly amusing.

"Do not touch her," both Lachlan and Murdoch hissed in unison.

"I think that is up to Miss Darrow," the Unseelie king said. Sorcha's blood ran cold.

"What is that supposed to mean?" she whispered, though she was beginning to understand full well what Eirian was insinuating.

His smile was so radiant that Sorcha momentarily forgot that she was dealing with a snake. "I believe you have already worked that out. If your life is so important to them, Miss Darrow, then I shall have it. A fitting punishment for the creatures who care for you so much."

Lachlan charged forward, but when his foe raised a hand some invisible force stopped him just shy of being able to touch Sorcha. "Clara, don't you dare agree to this!" he snarled. "Don't you dare –"

"I believe it is up to your lovely human paramour to decide what it is that she wants to do," Eirian said. "So what will it be, Miss Darrow: your life, or theirs?"

Sorcha took several seconds to reply, though in truth she needed no time at all to make her decision. Forcing herself to look past Lachlan, she locked eyes with Murdoch and opened her mouth to speak; he dropped to his knees before she uttered a single word.

"*No*," he mouthed. "Do not do –"

"I love you," she told him. "I love you. I love you. I've loved you all my life, even when I did not know who or what you were. Of course I will save you."

Murdoch did nothing but stare at her. Sorcha had just admitted her love for him in front of everyone, and he was staring at her the way he'd done on the plinth in the Seelie Court. There was no doubt about it: he had always loved her, too, as strongly and as deeply and as desperately as was possible for him to love another living being.

And so did Lachlan. Sorcha could see it now, though she had ignored the extent of his feelings and pretended that they were not truly serious for two years. He loved her, and she loved him.

It was simply a different kind of love than the all-consuming feelings she held for the kelpie.

"You know how I feel about you," she said to Lachlan, whose golden eyes were full of furious tears.

Since Sorcha could not fathom being able to live forever, giving up her life for Murdoch and for Lachlan seemed like the biggest gesture of her love for them that she could make. The biggest sacrifice a human was capable of.

She knew before either of them spoke that they would not let her do it.

CHAPTER THIRTY-TWO

Lachlan

Lachlan could only stare at Sorcha in disbelief. Not only had she admitted to loving the kelpie – a fear that had eaten away at Lachlan's brain for the past two years – but she was willing to give up her life for the monster.

And for him.

I will not stand for it, he glowered. *I will not. She cannot do it.*

"You will not give yourself up for me!" Murdoch called out, voicing his protests before Lachlan could even open his mouth. He turned his gaze to Eirian. "I will die, and gladly. Give me the most horrific death you can imagine, only let Miss Darrow go."

But the faerie merely laughed. "She has already voiced her consent. What can you do, kelpie? It turns out this mortal wields more power to control the two of you than I ever could. Except that her power is now *mine.*"

"You...you have no intention of killing her," Lachlan

stuttered, horrified as he realised what was actually going on. "You will use her to keep us in check, not as a means to punish us!"

"Why of course. I would never pass up an opportunity for more control, my poor fox king."

"Half."

Everyone stared at Sorcha, various expressions of confusion, anguish and interest upon their faces. She wiped the tears from her face, straightened her posture, then turned to face Eirian properly. Her eyes were dark and angry.

In all her silver splendour, she looked like an Unseelie queen.

"Half," she repeated. "If you will not kill me, then you can have just half my life. Lachlan had no hand in your kin's deaths and had no way to prevent them, as you have already heard. You have no grounds upon which to punish him."

Lachlan expected Eirian's features to contort in anger at being spoken to in such a way, or to strike Sorcha where she stood for being so bold as to make demands of the Unseelie king. Instead the grin on his face grew larger as he brought a thumb up to his teeth. He sliced it open on the edge of a sharp canine, then smeared the resultant well of blood across Sorcha's forehead.

"No, no, no," Lachlan mumbled, watching in horror as Sorcha's deal with the dark faerie was sealed. *She does not know what she has done. This is bad. This is impossible.*

This cannot be happening.

Behind him Murdoch remained on his knees, too

numb to speak. Lachlan hated him for his hand in Eirian's grand entrapment, but there was a small part of him that felt sorry for him.

The kelpie had never wished harm upon Sorcha. His love for her was genuine, and Lachlan could see his heart breaking in two. He could not resent the creature for his feelings – not when they were purer than Lachlan's had been when he'd first met Sorcha Darrow and intended to enchant her to be his forever.

Eirian finally let go of Sorcha, then, and she stumbled on bloodied, broken feet until Lachlan leapt forward to catch her. She was as numb as Murdoch was, face pale and blank but for the streak of blood upon her forehead that sealed her fate forever.

"You would do well to leave my realm now," Eirian said, still grinning his vicious grin. "Miss Darrow, you will hear from me in due time. I do hope you give me that song some day."

And with that the faerie disappeared, leaving Lachlan, Sorcha and Murdoch in the middle of a site of absolute carnage. Sorcha trembled in Lachlan's arms, but then he realised that he himself was shaking her.

"You fool," he muttered. And then, louder, "you absolute *fool*. Do you know what you have done?"

"I have saved both of your lives," Sorcha replied, voice muffled against Lachlan's chest. He pulled away from her enough that he could see her face; Sorcha avoided his eyes. "I would never have let him kill you."

"But now he has imprisoned you and can control us!" he shouted, stunned and infuriated by Sorcha's lack of understanding of the gravity of her situation. "That is worse than the kelpie and me dying –"

"Do not dare say that!" Sorcha fired back, a spark of life returned to her lovely, mismatched eyes once more. She glanced at Murdoch, who staggered to his feet, then back at Lachlan. "You may have such little disregard for your own lives, but you are more important that I am. You have the Seelie to rule over, Lachlan. And Murdoch...who else can I rely on to keep Loch Lomond and the Darrow land safe? King Eirian can have half my life – I give it to him gladly – if it means our home is left untouched. If it means the ones I love are free from his grasp."

"Sorcha –"

"And besides," she said, forcing a smile onto her face, "it is only thirty years at most. Thirty years is nothing."

"But those thirty years could be from now until your fifty-first birthday, or spread over every night from now until your death, or any iteration in-between!"

"And I give it *gladly*," Sorcha repeated. "Let me save the two of you for –"

But Sorcha's words were cut off as Murdoch wrenched her from Lachlan's arms, crushing her against him as if he never intended to let her go.

Lachlan did not stop him.

He knew exactly how the kelpie felt.

CHAPTER THIRTY-THREE

Murdoch

Despite the fact they were not alone, and that Lachlan himself was one of their onlookers, Murdoch could not tear himself away from Sorcha. He smothered her against his chest, wishing nobody else was around to lay their eyes or hands upon her.

"Just what have you done, you foolish girl?" he murmured into her hair; his voice cracked before he reached the end of his question.

Sorcha squirmed against him, struggling out of Murdoch's embrace just far enough that she could gaze up at him. It was plain to see that she was terrified by what she'd promised the Unseelie king, but there was something else in her eyes, too.

Determination. Conviction. Murdoch hated how familiar they were to see upon Sorcha Darrow's face.

"I would never have you nor Lachlan die for me," she said, resolute. She glanced at the faerie as he watched the pair of them in silence. A small smile curled her lips. "I've never been one to be saved by others."

"Sorcha –"

She held a finger up to Murdoch's lips. "No. Do not argue with me on this. What's done is done, as well you know."

When Murdoch turned to Lachlan it was clear the Seelie king was already thinking hard and fast about how to undo everything Sorcha had promised Eirian. *I guess we'll have to fight on the same side again...for a while,* he realised, not relishing the idea for even a moment.

When Sorcha kissed him softly Murdoch diverted his attention back to her. "I am all right with this, I swear," she said. "If I was given the choice again I would make the same decision in a heartbeat." She broke away from Murdoch's arms and held out a hand for Lachlan, who immediately took it. Going by the wince on Sorcha's face he was all but crushing her fingers, though she did not comment on the pain. "You both cannot be so eager to save me and not expect me to feel the same way in return."

Murdoch said nothing. Lachlan said nothing. Sorcha was right, and they both knew it. And yet still it hurt, for Sorcha was human and they were not. They had powers she could only dream of. They *should* have been the ones to protect her, not the other way around.

And yet we weren't. We couldn't. And if being a kelpie is not enough to keep Sorcha out of harm's way, then...

"Lachlan."

The faerie frowned at him. "What is it?"

"Can you take us back to the Seelie Court?" Murdoch asked, though he was thoroughly uncomfortable even thinking about being there again. But anything was better than the realm they were currently dwelling in. *Anything.*

With some reluctance Lachlan waved Murdoch over to his side and placed his hand on the kelpie's shoulder. His other hand was still wrapped around Sorcha's; she huddled in closer to the two of them on instinct.

"I suppose this will be much drier than leaping from loch to loch," she murmured wryly. If it wasn't for the situation they were currently in Murdoch might have laughed at her joke. Considering Sorcha's torn and bloodied feet, tear-stained face and unsettlingly beautiful, Unseelie ball gown, laughing was the last thing on Murdoch's mind.

Lachlan wiped the mark of the Unseelie king from Sorcha's brow and kissed the skin there, though no amount of washing away the dark blood would remove its curse. "You'll feel a touch light-headed, but that's it. Hold on tight."

And then, between one blink and the next, the three of them disappeared from the Unseelie realm and the haunting, plaintive music of the solstice revel to land right in Lachlan's bedroom.

Sorcha gasped and staggered; clearly the faerie's magic had affected her far more than it had Murdoch. He swept her away from Lachlan to sit down upon the golden, gauzy-curtained bed. The mere sight of it brought memories flooding back of when he had lain upon the mattress and Sorcha had sung him to sleep. Considering what she did to him the following day the memory was bittersweet; Murdoch was coming to accept that his entire relationship with the human woman he loved was going to follow a similar feeling.

Murdoch froze.

I love her. I haven't told her even once that I love her.

He knelt in front of Sorcha, tilting her chin until their eyes were level. "Sorcha," he began, "I –"

"Miss Sorcha?"

Suppressing a scowl, Murdoch turned to see the blonde-haired faerie, Ailith, standing in the doorway. She held a hand to her heart, eyes wide with surprise at the sight of all three of them. But then she smiled in relief. "I was so worried, Miss Sorcha," she said, closing the gap between them to rest a hand upon Sorcha's head. "Around ten minutes ago a group of Seelie arrived at my door and told me about what was going on – I was just about to leave for the revel myself! Oh, Miss Sorcha, you are in pain. Let me see to it."

Clearly she has no qualms about ordering me around, Murdoch thought when Ailith pushed him out of the way to tend to Sorcha's injured feet. He stood up, backing away until he was by Lachlan's side. The faerie glared at him.

"I still can't believe you let her be taken by the *Unseelie king,* you overgrown –"

"Lachlan, hush!" Ailith called out over her shoulder. "You and I both know fine well you intended to take Miss Sorcha along with you to the solstice revel. I am afraid King Eirian was destined to come into contact with her, no matter what either of you did."

"Ailith, he took *half her life,*" Lachlan muttered, outraged once more. "To save *his* skin –"

"And yours, as I recall," Murdoch countered, feeling very much like he wished to punch Lachlan in the face.

216

"And it's all the fault of your kind, anyway. If Sorcha had never –"

"Will you please stop *arguing*?!" both Ailith and Sorcha exclaimed in unison.

"What's done is done," Ailith said, though her sapphire eyes were endlessly sad.

Lachlan shook his head in frustration. "Why are you on her side? She is mortal. She is –"

"Very brave, and responsible for her own actions," Ailith cut in. "I thought you would have learned that by now, Lachlan. You should be more grateful to her for saving your life."

Ailith's words starkly reminded Murdoch of why he had asked Lachlan to take them all back to the Seelie Court to begin with, though now he was faced with what he had to say next he found his tongue had grown thick and dry in his mouth.

Then he caught Sorcha's eye and relaxed. For who cared if Murdoch had to ask a Seelie for help, if it would allow him to spend the rest of his life with her?

"Lachlan," he said, very quietly. "Ailith. I have a request."

Everyone stared at him; Lachlan's brows narrowed in immediate understanding. "You can't honestly expect us to abide by this request. You can't. Surely you can see that."

Ailith glanced at her king, then back to Murdoch. Then understanding dawned on her face, too, and she stood up. "Kelpie, that is serious indeed. Do you truly know what it is that you're asking for?"

Murdoch gestured at Sorcha, who was watching him

217

from the bed with the most confused expression he had ever seen upon her lovely, human features. *Of course I know what it is I'm asking for.* "She gave up half her life," he said. "All I want is to live that with her - as her equal."

"No!"

Sorcha had bolted upright and rushed to Murdoch's side despite her injured, bandaged feet, grasping at one of his hands with both of her own. "Murdoch, you can't mean that you want them to strip you of all your powers. You can't -"

"If you are allowed to do what you want with your life for me, then I am allowed to do the same," Murdoch said, smiling. He stroked the side of Sorcha's face; she closed her eyes in a moment of contentment. He locked his gaze on Lachlan. "Make me human. I beg you. I know what I ask is no easy magic to weave. I would not ask if there was some other way to do it."

"Such magic is irreversible, kelpie," Lachlan uttered. "Even if I *liked* you I would be disinclined to perform such a -"

"I love her. You know that."

Sorcha's eyes lit up at Murdoch's admission. Her grip tightened on his hand. "You love me," she mouthed, as if in wonder. "You really do. I do not know why I ever doubted that you did."

He could only laugh in disbelief at such a doubt. "Miss Darrow," he said, "I love you more than anything."

It was bizarre; before, it was Murdoch's use of Sorcha's given name that had caused her heart to accelerate and her cheeks to flush. Now it was her

218

surname. Murdoch knelt in front of her, lowering his forehead to rest it against Sorcha's hands. "All I want is to be with you," he said. "I have lived on this earth long enough to know I would be a fool to give up what we have."

Nobody said anything for a while. And then:

"Five years."

It was Lachlan who had spoken. Murdoch glanced at him out of the corner of his eye; the faerie had a calculated expression on his face, as did Ailith.

She nodded her agreement. "Yes, I think five years is more than fair."

"Five years for what?" Sorcha asked.

"For your kelpie to prove that he can truly live like a human," Ailith explained. "If he can do that, then we shall make him mortal."

Murdoch stood up, ready to protest. "But Sorcha might only –"

"It is precisely *because* she does not have a lot of time left that I'm demanding this," Lachlan said, face grave. "If Eirian makes a move over the next few years – which I imagine he will – then the Seelie Court will need your strength to help us. As a kelpie, not a man. And you *will* help us, or we won't help you."

Murdoch said nothing for a moment. He looked at Sorcha, whose mismatched eyes were a little too bright as she watched his face carefully for a sign of his decision. But of course he had already made it; five years was a small price to pay, after all.

He held out a hand to Lachlan. "Deal," he said, resisting the urge to squeeze the faerie's hand a little too hard when he shook it.

A slow grin crept across Lachlan's face as he broke from Murdoch's grasp to address Sorcha. "And in the meantime, Clara," he said, going back to using her false name simply to infuriate Murdoch, "if you ever get tired of your horse – which I don't doubt that you will – you know where to find me."

"Lachlan!" Ailith scolded.

But Sorcha merely laughed. She closed the gap between herself and Lachlan, stretching up on her tiptoes to brush a kiss against his lips. "I know," she whispered. Murdoch's heart tightened and twisted painfully, but then Sorcha added, "You are wrong about him, though, Lachlan. And me. I will not grow tired of him. And I think *you* have known that longer than even I have."

Lachlan sighed. "Do not make me have to admit the truth *in front of him,* lass."

"But then the two of you could be friends!" Sorcha said, voice full of mischief. "You could –"

"Absolutely not," Lachlan cut in, followed by the sound of Murdoch cursing under his breath at such an outrageous suggestion.

Sorcha giggled. "Far more impossible things have happened."

"In your dreams, perhaps," Lachlan scoffed.

Sorcha raised an eyebrow at him. "More of my dreams have come true than naught."

"Well if that wasn't a filthy proposition then I don't know –"

"Will the two of you be staying the night?" Ailith

interrupted, casting a worried glance at Murdoch in the process. But though Lachlan's relationship with Sorcha was something he could never profess to understand, and though the Seelie king delighted in saying just about anything to get a rise out of him because of it, Murdoch could not be angry with the ease of their flirtations.

Sorcha loved him. She loved the kelpie of Loch Lomond. That was enough.

Sorcha shook her head at Ailith, gave Lachlan a final kiss, then walked over to Murdoch's side. His hand found hers as if it was the most natural thing in the world. "No," she said, "I have a poor, *real* horse named Galileo who misses me. Where we have to be is far more important than the faerie realm."

She didn't have to say it out loud. Murdoch knew exactly where she meant.

In an area full of people who loved and depended on the Darrows. In a handsome, red brick house overlooking the loch. In a small gap between worlds, where kelpies fell in love with humans and mortal girls sang longingly to them through the water.

They were going home.

EPILOGUE

Eirian

The Golden King of the Seelie Court was running on borrowed time, and Eirian knew the faerie was well aware of it. A human had saved him, after all. A *human.* And not merely once, either.

Sorcha Darrow had foiled Eirian's attempts to dispatch with Lachlan twice.

It was supposed to have been simple: his brother, Innis, was already in love with Queen Evanna. That part Eirian had not planned but was instead happy coincidence. Or, rather, a sign from the fates themselves that they wished for the Unseelie king to hold dominion over all otherwordly creatures.

Innis had not taken much convincing to get behind his brother's plot to overthrow the Seelie Court. Evanna's only son and heir would never be ready to rule, he had said. He didn't have the right temperament. His own son was a much better fit for the crown alongside the kind and beautiful faerie, Ailith. Eirian had not argued on this point, merely encouraging his brother to keep Lachlan close at hand once it became apparent that his mother's health was failing.

When Evanna passed away Innis and Fergus' part of the job had been simple: get rid of the Seelie prince. A fox curse had been a stroke of genius – even Eirian could see that. His brother and nephew never needed to hide Lachlan's death, for they would not kill him. All they had to say was that the poor lad, anguished by his mother's death, had run away.

That was supposed to have been it. Fergus would take the throne of the Seelie Court, calm the faeries down after Evanna's death and her son's disappearance, and then...

Eirian would swoop in, kill both his brother and his nephew, and take the kingdom for himself.

So how had it transpired that Sorcha Darrow enchanted a kelpie to her side to kill Eirian's family first, then break Lachlan's curse to put him back on the throne? How had a *human* managed to undo years and years of planning?

And now she had stopped Eirian from getting rid of Lachlan once again, though the Unseelie king knew that the damage he could inflict upon his royal rival by taking half of Sorcha's life would be worth it in the long run.

Eirian had always been in it for the long run.

"*But tho' my despair is past curing,*" he sang, gazing out of his bedroom window as the beginnings of a blizzard obscured his entire kingdom from view. It was the last line of the song Sorcha had sung through the streets of London when Eirian had ordered his ghouls to frighten her right into his arms. He had almost spirited her away then and there out of sheer spite.

But there was something about the girl that was charming. Something that had given Eirian enough pause to not simply destroy her where she stood. She had a kelpie - the most powerful kelpie in all of Scotland - and the Seelie king under her thumb, after all. Though she was a human, she was valuable.

Now Eirian had big plans for her and the delicious fear and disgust he had seen in her eyes when she signed over half her life to him. He knew Sorcha had refused Lachlan's offer of immortality time and time again; when she'd agreed to Eirian's deal she'd clearly thought she was giving him no more than thirty years.

He was going to make that closer to forever.

"*But tho' my despair is past curing,*" he repeated;

"*And much undeserv'd is my fate,*

I'll show by a patient enduring

My love is unmov'd as her hate."

Yes, Eirian had always been in it for the long run, and he was going to drag Sorcha Darrow along for the ride.

THE STORY CONTINUES IN KING OF FOREVER...

Lachlan

It was raining, and Lachlan hated it. Under ordinary circumstances he would have deigned not to go outside, but today was different.

The last five years had passed like five minutes, and two months ago Lachlan celebrated his one hundred and fourth birthday. Now that he had lived a full century he could finally stand tall and true beside the older members of the Seelie Court, though by his kind's standards he was still very young indeed.

Especially to be king, as they keep reminding me, he thought dolefully. With the threat of war with the Unseelie simmering beneath the surface of every choice the Court made Lachlan had been subject to ever more criticism from his kin. He had been foolish to face up to Eirian with no way of winning against him, they said. They were right, of course, especially since the Unseelie king now had the worst kind of leverage against him.

That leverage was Sorcha Darrow.

But Lachlan could not find it in him to regret his feelings for the mortal woman, who was the reason he was standing outside in the rain, nor the hold she had over his heart. He loved her dearly, and deeply, in a way he might never admit aloud to anyone. His feelings for her cast a shadow over the love he held for his queen, Ailith, making it feel shallow and adolescent.

Though that may be because of her new consort. Lachlan pushed the thought away.

"Sometimes the mortals really do know how to put on a good funeral service."

Lachlan smothered a flinch of surprise at the voice, which belonged to his adviser, Ronan. The faerie was broad and burly, with curling horns like a ram's upon his head, though at present he was under the glamour of a human. Lachlan was, too, as were the rest of the faeries with him. For they were indeed at a mortal funeral: that of William Darrow.

Sorcha, whose usually wild hair was pinned back and impeccably tidy for once, stood by the edge of her father's grave with her bereft mother and her kelpie lover, Murdoch, by her side. A fine mist of winter drizzle enshrouded them all, causing their silhouettes to waver as if they, too, were made of water. When Margaret Darrow began to weep Murdoch swept her into his arms so that her tears could remain hidden from the rest of the funeral-goers.

Though it frustrated him that the kelpie had integrated himself into Sorcha's family in a way Lachlan could not, he kept his insecurities from showing on his face. He was not the kind of fool to interrupt the family during such a moment, after all, though Lachlan wanted nothing more than to console the woman he loved. No, he remained a polite distance away with his small cohort of faeries who wished to pay their last respects to the kind and loving human that was William Darrow.

The man had been keeper of the land around both the loch and the forest his entire life, protecting everyone from all manner of threats from greedy, selfish mortals. In his later years he had passed that duty onto his daughter due to his ailing health, thus keeping the Darrow tradition alive. The faeries owed a great deal to the family, though they knew humans in general were becoming a bigger and bigger threat against their supernatural way of life.

Sorcha and the kelpie's battle against Murdoch Buchanan's old work colleagues was chilling proof of that.

The beast wearing Murdoch's skin cast his eyes over to Lachlan. A curt nod passed between them, then the man who was not a man returned his attention to Sorcha and her mother. Lachlan reached a hand out across the graveyard towards Sorcha, thinking that perhaps it wouldn't hurt to say a few words to her, but Ronan gently touched his wrist to stop him.

"Leave her for now, Lachlan," he said, not unkindly. "Miss Darrow and the kelpie are coming to the Court this evening, are they not? Save your words and sympathies for then."

Yet Lachlan could not help but take a step or two towards Sorcha until his keen ears could pick up on the muffled sobs of Margaret Darrow through the rain as she cried against Murdoch's chest.

"He would have l-loved to see you two m-married," she wailed. Murdoch stroked her greying hair, keeping his eyes on Sorcha as she fought back tears herself. She could not bear to look at her mother, that much was clear. "A w-wedding and a child," Margaret continued, "wouldn't matter if the bairn was a b-boy or a girl. William was so good with children."

Something inside Lachlan twisted and coiled like a snake readying to strike. Whilst Murdoch was still a kelpie he could not father children with a mortal...but his final five years as a magical beast were up. Lachlan and Ailith had promised to change his very being permanently, and faeries always kept their promises.

There was just one thing Lachlan had to ask of Sorcha before he turned Murdoch human.

Tonight, Lachlan thought, as Sorcha's green-and-blue eyes caught his for just a moment before he turned for the forest with his companions. In them he saw all the anguish she was keeping at bay for the sake of her mother. She would cry later, he knew, perhaps when nobody was around. Lachlan loved her for it – the strength she held for other people in place of herself – though he also despaired because of it. It was the reason Sorcha was currently in such a dire situation, after all.

But Sorcha had long since made her decision to save the Seelie king and the kelpie of Loch Lomond at the price of half her life. There was nothing Lachlan could do about it now, except approach his mortal love with his most demanding request to date.

Tonight, he thought again as Ronan led him back into the cover of the forest. Once well hidden from the mortals at the funeral the faeries collectively let their nondescript human glamours drop, resulting in a whole host of strange and magical creatures left looking more bizarre than usual due to their uncomfortable, sombre mortal clothes.

Lachlan tossed one final glance over his shoulder in Sorcha's direction, though through the dense cover of winter pines he could no longer see her. *I will ask her tonight, whilst there is still time left to fulfil the request.*

He knew that Murdoch would not like what he was going to ask at all.

Ailith had remained at Court whilst Lachlan attended William Darrow's funeral, though the pale-skinned faerie was nowhere to be seen when he returned to the Seelie palace. *Her new lover is keeping her company, no doubt,* he thought, wasting no time in requesting a jug of blackberry wine from a passing servant on his way to the throne room. Lachlan was happy for Ailith – truly, he was – but seeing her with another was not exactly something he'd wished to witness over the past year.

And so it was that Lachlan was somewhere past tipsy when a silent-footed servant crept into the throne room to inform him that Sorcha and Murdoch had arrived. He was still in his mortal funeral clothes – largely all black, a colour Lachlan rarely wore – and his shoulder-length hair was in desperate need of a comb, but he did not care.

For what were appearances, in the face of the woman who could see right through them?

"Send them in," Lachlan said as he waved towards the servant, but in the time it took for him to speak the door was pushed wide open by Murdoch, closely followed by Sorcha. The kelpie was similarly still in the clothes he had worn to the funeral, though against his dark hair and coal-coloured eyes the ensemble did not look out of place in the slightest.

Sorcha, however, had changed into a familiar, forest-coloured dress with an intricately embroidered bodice that Lachlan adored. She had released her hair from its pins, too, and had clearly brushed through it until it shone going by the soft and lustrous way it tumbled down her back. She was a sight to behold, even with the slight tinge of red rimming her eyes suggesting she had indeed cried in the hours since Lachlan left her father's funeral.

Now I feel an idiot for not making an effort with my appearance for her sake, Lachlan thought glumly, rubbing a lock of bronze hair between his thumb and forefinger. *Though I suppose there is naught I can do about it now.*

Murdoch was the first to speak when he and Sorcha stopped in front of Lachlan on his gilded throne. He preferred the thrones that sat on the plinth outside in the revel clearing but given that it was January it was altogether much too cold to host such a meeting beneath the stars.

"What was so important that you had to call us here today, fox?" Murdoch demanded, though his voice was soft and gentle. For Sorcha's sake, Lachlan assumed, though given the kelpie's usage of his favourite insult *fox* he had to wonder what the point was of changing his tone. Either way, it didn't matter; Lachlan had to pose his request to Sorcha regardless of what Murdoch said or did over the next few, all-important minutes.

However, now that he was faced with what he had to ask Lachlan found that he could not look at Sorcha at all. He straightened on the throne, smoothing a hand over his hair and hooking a finger inside the uncomfortably restrictive collar of his human shirt as his brain fumbled for the right words.

"What I have to say – what I have to ask of you," he began, very slowly, "is no easy request. I am well aware of that. Yet I have thought on the matter at length over the past five years and find myself in a position where it would be detrimental to delay voicing my request any longer."

Murdoch frowned, deeply suspicious, though Sorcha's previously sad expression changed in a moment to one of curiosity. She closed the gap between herself and the throne to rest a hand over Lachlan's. Her skin was icy cold, sending a shiver down his spine. But the way Sorcha looked at him was warm and familiar and tugged at Lachlan's heart, forcing his request out of his mouth before he could do anything to stop it.

"Have my child."

Out now!

***

ACKNÖWLEDGEMENTS

Would you believe me if I said I uploaded the manuscript for this to Amazon five minutes before the deadline? Because that's what happened. As a result I would like to thank my colossal procrastination skills for nearly ruining this book and then ultimately saving it.

I hope you all enjoyed Lord of Horses! It was super interesting to bring Murdoch's point of view into the trilogy after him being the dark horse (ha!)/villain in Prince of Foxes. I'm excited to take things in an even more twisted direction in the final book, and explore more of my favourite tales (including Hades and Persephone, which is not Scottish at all, the horror!).

Writing more of a Gothic romantic fantasy was really fun. I definitely like my love stories dark and twisted!

I adore Lachlan with all my heart, but it was his turn to feel wretched this time around. Murdoch was miserable at the end of book one, after all. And Sorcha remains towing the bittersweet line between the two otherwordly creatures vying for her affections for whom she cares very much. Except now she has a wicked, Unseelie king to contend with! Will she have met her match? Just what is going to happen to our unlikely heroes? Will Ailith ever get a point of view?

I guess you'll have to stay tuned to find out.

I'd like to thank my wonderfully talented sister, Eva, for the song recommendations that I used as inspiration in Lord of Horses. I couldn't use them all in this book so you'll see some of them in King of Forever. It definitely pays to have a professional singer in the family!

Until next time,

Hayley

ORIGIN OF POEMS

The Kelpie (Nick Baker; 2010)

Lost is my Quiet (Henry Purcell; 1698)

Flow My Tears (John Dowland; 1596)

ABOUT THE AUTHOR

Hayley Louise Macfarlane hails from the very tiny hamlet of Balmaha on the shores of Loch Lomond in Scotland. After graduating with a PhD in molecular genetics she did a complete 180 and moved into writing fiction. Though she loves writing multiple genres (fantasy, romance, sci-fi, psychological fiction and horror so far!) she is most widely known for her Gothic, Scottish fairy tale, Prince of Foxes – book one of the Bright Spear trilogy.